I0537794

Gloria's Daughter

Ian Saul Whitcomb

Also by Ian Saul Whitcomb:

*I Married a Galaxy-Conquering
Alien Space Monstrosity*

Sexpossessed

ISBN: 0692353704
ISBN-13: 978-0692353707 (Wobbly Cockatrice Productions)

FOR ALL MOTHERS EVERYWHERE

Even the ones who, like my own, are not prostitutes.

CONTENTS

CHAPTER ONE

I just stood there blinking when the door opened and it wasn't Gloria.

"She'll be here in a minute," the girl said, already turning to head for the room's far exit. "Close that behind you."

Holy shit. She said she had a daughter, but she never said she was this hot.

"Wait, wait ..."

She turned, rolling her eyes, one hand on the knob of the interior door between the main house and this refurbished garage.

"What."

She had her mother's blue eyes, but colder, and long, straight, red hair several shades darker than Gloria's. Those eyes pulled mine away from her exquisitely curved body in its jean shorts and tee. I didn't want her to think I was a pig.

Except I realized, under her harsh blue stare, that I had nothing ready to tell her.

"Look," she said before my brain could produce words, "I don't want anything to do with ... *this.*"

Her gaze indicated the cozy little boudoir with a sweep, but didn't pause long enough to settle on anything.

"So if it's okay with you, I'm going to go now."

The revulsion in her tone – not just for me, but for what the room represented – finally gave me something to say. "She's a good person, you know. You don't have to approve of what she does, but she's a good person."

The auburn eyebrows lowered. "Fuck you. Of course I know she's a good person."

Then with a yank of the doorknob she spun and disappeared into the house.

I went to the corner loveseat and sat down, face burning. Why had I said anything? Why hadn't I just let her escape the moment she first turned away?

Because you are *a pig,* I thought. I'd seen that gorgeous hair, those long pale legs, the way her bottom firmly rounded out her daisy-dukes – and I hadn't wanted that vision to get away. I yearned to interact with such a thing of beauty, and of course to see more of her front with its fresh young face and soft breasts mounded up beneath the cottony whiteness of her shirt. *It wasn't enough to just stare at her ass as she left, you had to be a jerk and try to get more.*

Sound came in through the closed inner door, a raised voice: "... telling them about me now? ... hole acted ... knew something about me ..."

A softer noise followed, too low to hear the words, but undoubtedly Gloria's voice.

Then, "... don't give a shit how long ... fucking this guy ... my goddamn privacy!"

After a couple more indecipherable words from Gloria there came a pause, followed by the slam of a door somewhere at the far end of the house.

Then another pause.

When the knob turned, Gloria stood there in the black

silk kimono robe she almost always wore for me. She had no makeup on, and after the contrast of her daughter's youthful face, she looked lined and tired, even more than normal.

She smiled at me, though. Weakly, but with all her usual sincerity.

"I'm sorry about that," she said, moving in and pulling the door to behind her. "I really –"

"No. Fuck, that was totally my fault." I stood up scowling and steaming at myself. "If I'd thought two seconds, I'd have known she wouldn't want to talk to me. It was rude, and I shouldn't have opened my mouth. I'd ask you to apologize for me except then I'd just be intruding into her life again and making you the messenger."

Her smile deepened and she met me in the center of the room, pressing her face to my shoulder as we embraced. The silk of the kimono and the silk of her flesh underneath sent some of the tension flowing out of me. Her hands pulled tighter at me than normal, and we held each other longer before letting go. I took the time to breathe in the fragrance of her hair, that rich, healthy smell marketing guys wish they could put in commercials to sell more shampoo.

"I dropped a glass and then cut myself cleaning it up," she explained, showing me the band-aid across the base of her right thumb as her hand rose to shift a scarlet wave of hair from her forehead. "If it had been pretty much anyone else, I would have just let them wait outside, but she was right there and I knew it was you and –"

"Don't worry about it."

I had her hands in mine now, and she had her face tilted up to take me in with those blue eyes.

"So." She swung our hands out and in. "What do you

want to do?"

The loveseat had been very comfortable, and I couldn't get enough of how she looked in that robe. I nodded over one shoulder. "Have a glass of wine?"

She smiled and released my hands, trailing her fingers out of mine and sashaying backwards toward the standing bamboo screen in the far corner of the room. "Sure."

Settling myself back into the cushions, I listened to her rummage in the little micro-fridge she kept hidden behind the screen with her computer desk.

"How's your week been?" I asked.

"Okay," she said, with a sigh that admitted it wasn't true. I heard a cork, then wine glugging into one glass and another. "Not the best week I've ever had, I guess."

She came back out carrying two goblets of deep burgundy. "But it's getting better now."

Handing me my glass, she settled on the other end of the loveseat, one leg tucked up under her, the shimmering black robe gapping open down the front to reveal her sternum and the inner curves of her breasts. I felt heat in my stomach without even sipping the wine.

"How about yours?"

"Also getting better now," I said, reaching out with my glass to touch its rim to hers. We both drank, she a few more swallows than I. Her free hand made its way up my arm where it rested along the back of the sofa, fingers teasing at the hair there, then smoothing the hem of my shirtsleeve.

"Why can't everything be this easy?" she asked, her eyes seeking the answer in my face.

I shrugged. "Some things just fit nicely and other things just don't."

Gloria's eyes darted back toward the door into the house. Then she nodded in acknowledgment and took another long sip of wine.

"Are you all right?"

She laughed and leaned her torso forward, bringing her palm up to my cheek and giving me a clear view of her down-hanging breasts through the widening gap of her robe.

"Oh, Denny, you're always so concerned. I'm fine. And in just a few minutes, I'm going to be fantastic." She tweaked a flame-red eyebrow up with that last bit, and surging forces inside me washed away my sense of worry over her mood.

I leaned forward too and put my mouth on hers. Despite the wine and a hint of toothpaste or mouthwash behind it, I could taste that she was smoking again. But the clutch of her hand at my collar kept me from thinking about it too hard. Her tongue played a game of hide and seek with mine and her lips sealed my mouth with a heat that almost seared.

She was breathing hard when we pulled apart. All the weariness had left her face – her eyes shone lucent and intense.

"You'd better come up with some really good conversation or else take me to bed," she said.

"I've already screwed up at least one attempt at conversation today."

She knocked back the last of her wine, set the glass on the floor and rose to her feet, pulling me after her by the shirtfront. I managed to get my glass to the end table, still half-full, as she expertly unfastened my belt. By the time I got out of my shirt, Gloria had my pants and boxers down, then held each of my shoes firmly in turn to help me step out of them. The sash of her robe had come free while my shirt blocked my view, and now she flipped the kimono open and around her shoulders by its lapels to let the silky fabric flow from her arms to the floor.

I could only marvel at her as she knelt there before me, hands on thighs, eyes locked on my face. This woman might have been a hard-worn thirty-five or well preserved in her mid-forties. I had never asked her, but her college-age daughter and the fact that I'd been coming to see her for over ten years suggested it was more on the latter end. Her breasts gave downward a little more than when I'd first nervously entered this room. Her tummy swelled out farther, and her thighs had gained an inch or two. But she wasn't yet fat or droopy. And the creases at the corners of her eyes, and the bags under them, hadn't gotten so deep that she couldn't hide them with a little makeup when she wanted to look younger. She had a spattering of freckles at the bridge of her nose, a few more between and edging out across her breasts.

She looked so real like this. So completely sexual. And so glad to be with me.

Her right hand lifted from her thigh, her eyes broke from mine, and with a simple, easy motion her grip surrounded my shaft and her lips parted and rode softly up and around my tip. I'd been hard from the moment she took hold of my belt buckle; now I burgeoned to that incredible stiffness you can only appreciate before sex begins, when all your vitality seems concentrated into hardening that beam. Gloria's blue eyes closed. Nothing moved but her tongue, caressing the belly of my glans. Her breathing remained quick and shallow. A low moan vibrated out of her throat and through my penis.

Pulling back, she looked up at me and milked my cock with her hand, one stroke only.

"What do you want?" she breathed.

"Anything," I said. "Everything."

She shot her head forward, sucking me all the way in

and flattening her fingers against my belly. I felt her lips work insistently at the root of my cock, felt her esophagus constricting the far end, felt her tongue and her drawn-in cheeks all in between. Then she yanked away with a gasp, leaving a strand of saliva hanging between her mouth and my pulsing, teased cock. Her grip pumped tight along my spit-slick length as she returned her stare to my face.

Twice more, the same way: all the way down, hold, hold, hold, all the way off, popping her lips on the release.

Then she went down and bobbed, steadily, every wet, plush part of her mouth gliding and delighting the length of my cock.

"Jesus, Gloria," I gasped. She laughed around me, gobbling, licking, sucking. Her fingertips brushed against the circumference of my ball-sack, gentle and evenly spaced, whispering up and inward, down and out and around, to a slower rhythm than her sluicing, sleeving mouth. "Fuck, honey, you're going to make me come already ..."

She pulled off, and now her laugh came out cleanly without my cock to impede it. "Den, you know me better than that."

Getting up, her hand still wrapped around my dick, she rose on tiptoes to kiss me again, free arm going around my neck, breasts nestling against my chest. Then she kissed her way along my jaw and whispered in my ear, "You're going to come inside me, and before you do I'm going to make it last and last until you're all but crazy."

I stood there, eyes closed, holding her as she pumped my cock with firm, rotating strokes. The entire rest of the world faded away except for her hand, her breasts, the muscles of her back beneath my arm, her lips along my neck and her whispers rolling promises of pure ecstasy through my head. Slowly she tugged me toward the bed, turning us through a slow pirouette, then pressing harder against my front and kissing to urge me back, and back, until my calf brushed the satin-sheeted mattress and I lifted one leg and then the other to kneel atop it. Gloria kept her lips locked with mine and her hand around my erection as we moved up onto the bed – me easing down to lay my head into the pillows, her following to crawl into place above me.

She broke the kiss and sat up, straddling me just shy of my groin so that her hand gripped my hard-on right at the juncture of her thighs. I opened my eyes to watch her.

Her left hand spider-skated around my bellybutton, massaging the paunch I could never quite seem to exercise away. Her right cupped itself around the front half of my erection, so that the underside of my cock pressed into the abdominal softness just over her clean-shaved groin.

Her hips rolled, thighs pressing down on mine, hand and belly swaddling my cock in pleasure.

"How's that?"

"Good," I said, cupping her knees with my hands, then caressing up the gloss of her legs to her still-moving pelvis. "Terrific. Like always."

"Tell me when you're ready."

I nodded but didn't say anything yet. We watched each other, the only sounds our breathing and the faint noise of skin on skin and skin on sheets, murmuring to her movements. She still looked tired, but happy – maybe as happy as I felt. A slick film spread down between the tip of my cock and her stomach as the intensity of my hard-on brought viscous clarity welling up and out.

I could totally get there like this, I thought. More and more slick fluid would bead and flow from me. Gloria's fingers would press me more firmly against the lush swell of her tummy, while kneading and working the upper surface of my shaft. She would cycle her hips faster and faster, and the combination of those sensations and the look in her eyes would coax me into orgasm and bliss. But while she would enjoy it – and I would be overwhelmed by it – her pleasure would be personal and emotional, not raw and sensual. And I would feel selfish.

"I'm ready," I said.

With a smile, Gloria lifted up onto her knees and edged forward by inches, rubbing the glossy, lubed head of my dick along and down her stomach as she went. When it reached her mons, she parted her upper labia with the bulb and circled it round and round her clit. By now her left hand had moved up to my shoulder to support some of her weight as her upper body leaned forward and over me. Red waves of hair dangled down around her face, just long enough to tickle my upper chest and throat if she dipped her head.

Trapping her lower lip between her teeth, she maneuvered my cockhead into place at her slit, where I felt her heat and wetness. Ever so slowly, she pressed down with her hips, cunt kissing and then parting for my swollen tip, enfolding me, sinking her groin steadily toward mine as she swallowed me into and into and into herself. The damp fingertips of her right hand crept up my belly and across my chest now that she no longer needed them to direct our penetration.

Finally she settled fully and firmly into place, the mouth of her pussy flush and tight at the root of my cock, the ridge of her pubic arch driving her clit hard up against me. This was a moment I could never get enough of – Gloria all above and around me, motionless, warm, smiling, breasts and hair hovering inches from my skin. I slid my hands from her pelvis and waist up and around to her ass, full and fleshy and pillow-soft.

"Is there anyone you want me to be tonight?"

Some ineradicable caveman instinct annoyed me by flashing her daughter's image through my brain. We usually role-played every third session, maybe fourth, one fantasy or another – sometimes just me closing my eyes and picturing whatever hot chick I might have seen and drooled over recently, sometimes more elaborate and interactive scenarios. But I didn't want that tonight, and I certainly didn't want to bring her daughter into it. In the abstract, she'd probably think it was funny – Gloria's had plenty of opportunity to become jaded about male depravity, and it's pretty hard to surprise her. But I had seen the strain of their relationship in both of their faces just a second ago. That was not going to make a good ingredient for hot sex between the two of us now.

"I want you to be you, Gloria." And I really did mean it, even if I couldn't help marveling over how much she and her daughter resembled one another.

"Okay," she said, smiling. "Here's some Gloria for you, then."

Without moving, she started to fuck me – tightening the muscles deep in her vagina, relaxing them, tensing and releasing the ones along the middle of my shaft, squeezing me hard at the spot just behind her pubic bone, and then starting over again from inside. This created a slow roll along the length of my cock from tip almost to root. She's always had great control of those muscles, but she developed this particular trick sometime after we met, and it's only gotten better over time.

A moan ghosted up from my diaphragm. I gripped the round rich flesh of her bottom more tightly.

"You like?"

"Of course."

"And how about this?" The tail end of her spine flexed,

taking our merged sweet-spots through a tiny, beautiful orbit. Inside her, the vaginal contractions continued brilliantly along my shaft.

"Ohhhhh, yes. Do that again."

She did.

"And some more."

The swirling caress of her groin widened, grew constant, and joined with a new movement, her whole body easing forward and back atop me, drawing my cock out and feeding it back in at intervals synchronized with her rotations and the internal fondling by her cunt.

"God *damn*, Gloria."

"Fuck me," she demanded, now riding me in earnest.

"Oh, shit, yes." I pulled her to me, one hand still on her ass, the other up between her shoulder blades, pressing, holding as I thrust up in return to her steady grind. The swollen mouth of her pussy dripped its slick, wet treasure down along my girth onto my scrotum and into my pubic hair. I could feel her drenching me with every thrust.

"*Uhhh, Denny, yehhhsss ...*"

Her mouth dropped to my neck, tongue constricted to a slippery, insistent point that scrawled saliva along the track of my jugular to my earlobe, which she nipped and then sucked as she quickened her pace. Forward and back and forward and back she rocked in my arms, devouring me in the clenching tube of her vagina, driving her engorged clit against our juncture.

"Uh!" Just minutes into it, a panting, moist breath nestled into my ear as her lips parted and let the earlobe free. "There – Denny – "

"Mmmmm-*hhm*mm."

" – Denny – Oh, *God* – "

She stiffened above me, her rhythm suddenly spasmodic.

"UHHH! Yes, *fuck* me!"

I did my best to pound it up into her as her head and crotch both thrashed.

"Yes, Christ, I'm coming – hh – hh – *fuuuuck!*"

Her cunt twitched and vibrated around me, gushing, throbbing. The groan that went along with it could have been faked by any decent actress, but I doubted even Gloria had enough control to mimic that incoherent physical reflex cascading through the length of her vagina. As it trembled its way to stillness, she fell down onto me, limp, her mouth finding mine and slathering kisses across it.

"Mm, Denny, mlbll, mmgnuhh ..."

I rolled us over, staying inside all the way, sealing her lips with mine and taking my turn at control. Gloria's legs fell open to either side of me. Her breasts, now parted by gravity, heaved with her breath and glistened under a sheen of perspiration. I kissed her, pulling a few inches out and then slowly re-entering. The tight clutch of cunt-flesh had disappeared with the end of her orgasm; she now parted delicately around me as I slipped deeper. My sweat rolled down my sternum to join with hers, slicking and lubricating us so that our bodies glided almost as easily as our genitals.

"You're so amazing," I breathed into her ear. When I raised my head again, I saw her smiling, eyes closed, her face wonderfully sated. Lower, I felt her hips begin to work with mine in graceful, wavelike rolls. Neither of us moved with the power we'd used before, keeping things slow instead, enjoying the languid connection where our bodies met and meshed.

Her eyes opened and examined mine. She brought a hand up and trickled the fingers through my hair.

"Do you want me to come again?" she whispered. And she did mean come, not pretend to come.

I waited a few gentle strokes before answering.

"I can never get enough of you coming. But I want to do what you want."

She put both hands to my cheeks, then traced down with her fingertips to grasp my shoulders. Her feet came up to hook around my thighs just below the buttocks.

"I want to feel you throbbing big spouts of jizz into me."

"Okay," I said, smiling. "I can probably manage that. But what happened to making it last so long that I'd go crazy?"

"I'll do that on our second go."

I kissed her again, then drew further back and put a little more vim in my next thrust. Her cunt muscles came back to life, squeezing down around my penetration and sucking at me on my next slide out.

"Ooh," I said. "Nice."

Gloria licked her lips. "Do it like you mean it."

"Hey, I meant that."

"Mean it harder, lover."

We accelerated quickly then, working up our heat and speed. She kept her eyes fixed on mine, even as exertion started to rush her breathing, quiver her nostrils, force open her mouth in a pant. The flickering musculature of her vagina electrified each stroke I made into her, let loose a volcanic heat to seep out from the root of my cock, through my balls, up into my belly and down into my thighs. Sweat rolled and dripped from me, spattering her throat and then one cheek. I rose up, pushing, pumping, shoulders and head back for fear I'd sweat into her eyes. Orgasm barreled toward me, urgent and animalistic, wrenching a grunt from my throat as I hammered into her – then another, then another.

"*Ah!* Ah! Yes ..."

Her face lit up as she watched mine.

"Yes ... here it is ..."

Thrustthroughsqueezingcuntflesh, thrustthrust, thrust –

"AH! FUCK!"

Climax exploded through my body, across all my senses, out from my head to scatter my brain across continents. Distantly, I felt Gloria's heels hooked beneath my ass, pulling me tighter. Everything shimmered in time to the disgorging spout of my orgasm. My eyes shut, blinked open, shut, blinked open ...

Then the fresh, smooth face of Gloria's daughter swam across my vision in time to an ebbing gush, superimposed over her older, wiser features. My eyes squinched tight, and I was coming into that young woman's pussy, filling her womb with my seed.

"*UHHH!*"

I collapsed, and the image vanished, and there was only Gloria, soft and welcoming beneath me, legs relaxing, feet brushing their way gently down my thighs and then my calves, hands at the nape of my neck and teasing the hair on one arm.

"There you go, darling," she whispered. I lay still, considering whether to feel guilty about that sudden fantasy of her troublesome, lush teenager. But the orgasm had been too good, and I felt so close to Gloria now, and so at peace; the guilt couldn't work up the nerve to show its face.

"Woosh," I said at last. "I guess I should get off and uncrush you now."

Her fingers curled until the knuckles rubbed lightly from the base of my skull down the curve of my neck. "I can be crushed a little longer. I don't want you out yet."

"Mmm." Lifting up, I watched her face a moment and decided that when she said she didn't want me out, she was expressing a need, not a mere desire. The usual hierarchy of concern for Gloria, when we were together, went from my needs to my desires to her desires to her needs. She didn't reveal the last very often. "So what's wrong? You seemed really stressed before we got that wine in you."

She wiggled her hips. "You mean before we got you in me."

"Stop, I'm being serious. You looked ... tired. And you're smoking again."

"Shit." Her nose wrinkled. "I fooled myself into thinking the mouth rinse and wine would hide it. What a dodo."

"You can have one if you want. I don't mind." I said it with my thumb idly stroking the hollow above her collarbone. But she shook her head.

"I've already had two today, and I'm trying to hold it to that. Plus, some of my other regulars hate it, and I don't want to stink up the linens and mattress for them."

"You could get one of those e-cigarettes."

She rolled her eyes. "What, and turn myself into even *more* of a nicotine fiend? Are you trying to be a bad influence?"

"No." When the eye-roll finished, I kept my gaze on hers, which was blue and deep and completely lacking in any inquisitorial curiosity. She wasn't trying to figure me out. As far as I could tell, her gaze held nothing but appreciation. "I just don't like seeing you unhappy. But I won't pry if you don't want to talk about it."

Sighing, she put a hand in her hair and fluffed it out across the pillow under her head. Then she shrugged. "You know. Sometimes this is the best job ..." Her other hand moved up my arm to rest on my shoulder. "... but sometimes it's not. And for some reason it's harder with ... her home for the summer. Harder than when she lived here full-time. I think going away to school let her put this out of her mind. Maybe she got used to going weeks or months without having to remember her mother's a whore."

"Don't use that word."

She laughed. "It's just a word, Denny. All the words for it sound the same to me anymore. Except 'whore' sounds a little more honest, I think."

"Well, it sounds to me like you're running yourself down, and you've got no reason to do that."

Her hand came round to my chest, one fingertip circling to curl the chest hair around itself. She said nothing, but her smile thanked me. Then she looked past me to the ceiling, expression neutral and contemplative. I waited, felt her chest emptying and filling beneath mine through several deep breaths. The last one went out decisively.

"I had to tell a regular I couldn't see him anymore."

Her eyes came back to mine, serious.

"Did he do something?"

"Yeah."

A few seconds passed. Her hand dropped away from my chest and came to rest on the pillow next to her head.

"He's a choker. He likes me to say no and push at him a little when we're getting started, and then he puts his hands around my neck and tells me to be still. It's always been harmless – he doesn't use much pressure, and he's always nice when he's getting dressed afterwards. Complimentary."

I stroked her hair, soft and clean, though not as silky as when I'd first met her and we were both still young.

"So ... this time he's fucking me with his pants on and just pulled down. And he keeps getting almost there but not quite, and I can tell he's frustrated. His fingers start squeezing tighter than normal, but I don't say anything because I don't want to break his concentration and blow the orgasm for him."

A tremor of emotion vibrated through her. Most of my weight was on my elbows, so I couldn't really hug her. But I brought my arms into closer contact.

"And then suddenly he just stops and lets go. I ask him what's wrong, but he doesn't say anything. He's reaching down and tugging at his pants or something and I ask him what he's doing and he says, 'I'm gonna put my belt around your neck.' I tell him no, I'm not doing that, but by this time he's got the belt loose and he's bringing it up and I try to block it with my hands, but he's a big guy, really strong – so I have to say my safe word.

"And he ignores it."

"Jesus, Gloria ..."

"He's looping the belt around my neck and I say it again and by now I'm actually fighting him and he's panting and he starts to pull the belt tight and I scream it, one last time. And he goes still and looks at me and starts crying. He says, 'Oh my god, Lola' – that's what he calls me, Lola, 'you don't think I'd really hurt you, do you?' And I say, 'I never thought so before, but I had to say the safe word three fucking times and now I don't know, Harry.' I don't tell him my hand was already going up here ..." She patted the top edge of the mattress where I knew she had a couple of hanging pouches with things to protect herself. "... and I definitely don't tell him I was thinking about skipping the mace and going straight for the gun. So he lets go of the belt and says, 'Can I just finish? I won't even pull on it. I think I can get there just looking at it and pretending.' Anyway, his tears are dripping down all over me and for some reason I believe him and I say okay.

"He was right, it was over pretty quick from there, just a couple of minutes of him pumping and red-faced and staring at the belt around my neck. I could see his mouth moving, but he wasn't saying anything out loud, and I'm probably glad, because from the look on his face whatever he was saying in his head was pretty ugly. Then he looked away and shoved in hard and grunted and came and we were done. And when he got his clothes on, I told him we were done, done. He apologized again and paid and left."

"Good God. That's awful. I don't know how guys can –"

"And the worst part is ..." She was really shaking now. "...while he was there on top of me, grimacing and humping and imagining how it would feel to strangle me with a belt, I was thinking, 'Shit, this is eight hundred bucks a month I'm about to lose.'"

I tried to think of something to say. *What a bastard* didn't cut it. *Well, keeping yourself safe is the most important thing* might be true, but wouldn't pay any bills. And I for damn sure couldn't say, *I have plenty of money. Pencil me in for all his appointments.* It would sound like I was taking advantage of the fact that this guy basically strangle-raped her. *Not that she would call him a rapist,* I thought. *She consented to everything but the belt around her neck, and he stopped that after the third 'no.'*

What finally came out was, "You should cut my discount."

"What? No, that's – I can make it up with other clients, maybe some more online stuff – I wasn't fishing for anything, I'm not going to –"

I put my forehead down against hers. "At least until you fill up your schedule. It's not like it would break the bank, and it's not like I'm volunteering to make up the whole eight hundred." *Which I would totally do if I thought you'd take it.* "You can't tell me something like that and then not let me help."

With a peck on my lips, she told me, "You *are* helping. You're listening. Who else am I going to tell this to? My friends don't know what I do. My daughter? *That's* going to get me some sympathy. And I cut my therapist out when the tuition bills started coming in. Shit, I shouldn't be taking back your discount, I should be paying you the therapy fee. Or at least the copay."

I smiled a little but couldn't quite laugh. *Okay, well if you won't cut my discount, why don't I come another time or two a month? Come on, have the balls and say it.*

"What if –"

"Denny."

"Yeah?"

"You have been a stable spot in my life and a shining light in my schedule three times a month for twelve years. And I'm pretty sure I could get you to do any goddamn thing I wanted if I asked. I could wrap you so tight around my little finger that I'd get gangrene, and then I could get you to give me one of your fingers for a transplant."

I felt my face go red and fall into a stupid look. She completely had my number.

Putting a hand up to my cheek, she went on, "I didn't tell you so you could do something. I told you so you would *feel* something, and I would see you feel it, and I would know that Harry and his belt didn't matter. And now they don't. So you're going to keep getting your discount and I'm going to figure out how to make up the eight hundred bucks – and you're going to trust me that if I can't do it, if I'm stuck and desperate and there's no other way, I'll ask you to help. Okay? If I need to, I *will* ask."

Whatever the orgasm had done to my body and brain a few minutes earlier, those words put it to shame. I couldn't even speak.

Gloria patted both my shoulders simultaneously.

"Now get off of me and I'll get up and pee, and then I can come back and suck this beautiful cock back to life so I can keep that promise about making you crazy."

* * *

By the end of my two-hour time-slot, she'd made good on her prediction and then some. I lay blissfully on my back with her astride me and pressed flat to my chest, head beside mine on the pillow.

"Almost time," she sighed. The quarter-hour chime had sounded just before she finally let me come.

I opened my mouth to say maybe I should upgrade to three-hour sessions. But then I shut it again, not wanting to get back into the debate from our between-fucks interlude. Instead I slid my hand all the way down her spine, from between the shoulder blades to just above her tailbone, where I gave her a little pat.

"Look at it this way," I said. "'Almost time' means 'almost time to start looking forward to next week.'"

She kissed my cheek. "Is that how you look at it?"

"Three Mondays a month when eight o'clock closes in."

Her head came up, chin balancing on her knuckles where her hand cupped my shoulder. "What can I do special next time? Something I can spend the week thinking about and getting ready for."

Oh fuck.

"I don't know. I think ... uh ... I mean there's not really –"

She started laughing, just a low giggle at first, but growing and persistent enough to make both of our bodies shake before she got it under control.

"Oh, ha, this is going to be good. What has that naughty brain of yours cooked up that you're too embarrassed to tell me, after all this time?"

I frowned as if I didn't like being teased, but in reality that was the perfect response to free me up from my nerves and make me think I could actually ask her.

"All right, there's something. I'm just worried it will cross a line."

Patting my cheek, she said. "Honey, I don't think you have it in you to cross my lines — or even figure out how far out they are. Tell me. Whatever it is, we're going to have a *great* time with it."

So I told her.

* * *

The following Monday I got off work a few minutes earlier than normal, and traffic moved remarkably smoothly, and I found myself approaching Gloria's neighborhood at twenty to six instead of my normal five till. So I did what I normally do when I'm early and went to the corner gas station to blow a little time. I knew from casual conversation that Gloria always kept an hour's buffer between appointments, to get the sheets changed, tidy the room, shower and freshen herself up — and especially, to make sure her clients didn't cross paths. Even so, I always worried about the possibility of pulling up through the alley behind her street and finding some other car in the driveway, a guy with his seat leaned a little back and his eyes closed, afterglowing from an hour or two or three of what I was about to enjoy. The image made my stomach flip — and worse yet was the idea that he'd notice me, lift his head and give a grin and a thumbs-up before pulling away. More realistically, though less disturbing, I didn't want to risk her hearing my car roll up and feeling like she had to rush to let me in early.

For peace of mind, then, and out of simple courtesy, I stopped and topped off my tank (which didn't need it), checked all my tires and fluids, and then headed into the station's convenience store, meaning to clean the car-grime off my hands in the restroom.

But as I reached for the door handle, it swung out at me instead, and I had to jump back to keep from getting hit.

And there she was.

She looked up from fumbling the keys out of her purse, opened her mouth reflexively to apologize, and then froze when she recognized who she'd almost conked with the door.

Crap. What do I say? Duh, asshole, you say you're sorry like you told Gloria you wanted to last week.

"Look," I said, raising my hands in what I hoped was a conciliatory gesture, "I apologize for the other day. You were nice to let me in, and I should have just left it at that."

She made a sound in her throat. I couldn't tell if it was a grunt of acceptance or a growl. Her face looked resentful. "I wasn't being nice. I was just letting my mom push me around. You could have waited."

"I could have, and I'm —"

Another customer approached the store, and she stepped out to let the woman pass. When the door swung shut again, a little of the harsh edge had left her expression.

"Just — let's drop it, okay? Mom was really mad at how I acted. She guilt-tripped me all through dinner about you being one of the good ones, and if that's true then maybe I shouldn't have been such a bitch — whether or not I believe there's such a thing as a 'good one.'"

"You *should* believe it," I said. Hearing that Gloria had talked about me warmed something up in my chest, and made me want even more to make her daughter shed some of this disgust and judgment. "I'm not going to speak for myself, but she's told me before she has a lot of clients she actually likes. She says she'd have to change jobs if she didn't."

"Whatever. Anyway, if she's right then I'm sorry. Shit,

you guys are paying for my college education, so I guess I ought to be sorry regardless. I just can't stand the idea of her being used like that."

The door jingled behind her again, someone coming out this time. I moved farther to the side. She stepped that way too, but looked as though she meant to cut things off and duck away to her car. For some reason, I didn't want to let her.

"You go to a hair stylist, don't you?" I asked. "Does it feel like you're using her? Him?"

"What? Are you seriously saying getting my hair done is like —"

"How about a pedicure? Have you had one of those? Someone having to touch your feet, trim and buff all the calluses and crap off them?"

A little doubt crept into her face.

"Do you think there aren't people who go to your pedicurist with their feet all sweaty, smelly, lint between the toes?"

"That's ..." But she just let it trail off.

"And if you find a stylist you like, a manicurist or a pedicurist who's really good, don't you want to stick with them? Don't you talk to them, get to know them, at least a little? Don't you think of them as people? Maybe even friends after you've been going long enough?"

These were Gloria's metaphors, but I could see from her expression that she hadn't heard them before.

"That's fucked up. That's a fucked up comparison."

I shrugged. "Maybe it is for girls, and maybe even for most guys, but it's not for me. It's not fucked up at all. Your mom does something wonderful for me, and it's something she enjoys. And it could be just a transaction for either one of us or both, but that's not who we are. You don't really think that's who she is, do you?"

"No, because I don't think ... what she does, is who she is. And –" She drew herself up. "– sooner or later, if I had a hair stylist who was as great a person as my mom is, I'd start dropping hints for him to ask me out. I mean, if he wasn't gay. But I bet asking her for a date isn't high on your list of things to do with Gloria."

That face, so beautiful, so like her mother's, so full of challenge, made me want to say more – to prove something to her, to soften that look of cold triumph and maybe even warm the atmosphere between the two of them. There was only one thing I could think of to do that, though, and if it had just been about me, I probably would have dropped it and let her walk off feeling victorious. But it wasn't just about me.

So I said, very quietly, "How afraid would you be that your stylist wouldn't end up asking you, and then if you asked he'd say no, and you'd feel rejected, and you'd never be able to look at that salon as a wonderful, comfortable, welcoming part of your routine again? How afraid would you be that every time you got your hair cut after that, you'd be reminded about blowing your ability to regularly laugh and chat and share things with this terrific person while they did something nice for you?"

Her brows furrowed, disbelieving. "Are you telling me you'd actually consider – that you could pay her money, know about other guys paying her, and you'd still –"

"I'd rather leave it hypothetical," I said. "And I'd rather you didn't let her know I said anything like that."

"Yeah? Why not?"

I shrugged. "You don't get where I am today without having been hurt. So it's not simple or easy at all to think about changing. And what I have now with your mom *is* simple and easy – and beautiful, whether you believe that or not. The fact that it's partly a business arrangement doesn't keep it from being human and respectful, and it doesn't keep me from seeing her as a person, and being glad I have such a great person in my life. So I'd appreciate you letting us have what we have. But more importantly, I'd really like you to be able to see her the way I see her. She deserves that."

Her lips squeezed tight, and her face became a snapshot definition of the word "conflicted." She took a couple of sharp breaths through her nose.

Then she said, "I have to go now."

And that was it.

* * *

When Gloria opened the door, I just stood there a second, blinking back deja vu. She'd straightened her hair, I don't know, with a flat-iron or some kind of hot comb, and she had on the exact same tee shirt and shorts her daughter had worn the week before.

I'm betting she didn't get permission to wear those.

Her makeup was the same too, eye-shadow and blush identical shades, applied like she'd taken a picture to use as a guide, or like they'd dressed up their faces side-by-side in front of the same mirror.

Also not likely, I thought.

What she had down the best, though, was the expression. Absolutely indistinguishable from the one that had greeted me at this door the week before, and that had settled into place outside the convenience store once the surprise had worn off: icy and truculent. If it weren't for the height difference, I might actually have needed a second to recognize which one of them it was.

"Wow," I said. "How did you get here so fast from the gas station? Where's Gloria?" I didn't add, *And how did you get changed so fast.* Too unrealistic, and it might muddle up the information I was feeding her to improvise off of.

A flicker in the blue of her eyes said she was processing my words. Then the resentful teenager returned.

"I *knew* this was where you were headed," she crowed. "I knew it, and I'm sick of this shit, so I took the short way round and called Mom on the way and told her I'd broken down outside of town on the drive back to school. It'll take half an hour for her to realize I'm not really on the side of the road, and another half-hour to get back. So I guess it looks like your appointment is shot, Mr. Douchey. How do you like *that*?"

I wanted to compliment the performance – although it was still mid-summer, so the back-to-school scenario was a stretch – but I put on my own glare instead.

"How do I like it? I'm pissed, is how. I pay in advance for the month, Miss Smarty-pants. And now that you've wasted my time, your mom's going to have to double up for me or cough up a refund. Maybe I can even use this as leverage to get her to do some of the stuff she usually doesn't like."

Two kinds of fire flared in her eyes at that – a libidinous heat that was all Gloria, swamped after an instant by an excellent imitation of searing anger.

"You wouldn't ... what a pig!"

I stepped closer and put my hand on the doorframe. "I would. Unless maybe you want to make it worth my while not to."

She gave back a little, widening her eyes. "What – what do you mean?"

Now I moved into the frame, looming up close and grasping the edge of the door with my other hand, as if to keep her from slamming it on me.

"I think you know what I mean."

"You – oh my God, you've got to be kidding. There's no fucking way, you asshole."

Shrugging, I said, "Okay. I can take it out on Gloria if you want. And then I guess she can decide whether she wants to cut back your allowance or something."

"So I'm supposed to be your whore for some allowance money?" Her jaw clenched and she put some force against the door like she was testing my strength. I didn't let it budge.

"No, what you were *supposed* to do was drive your pretty little ass to school and let your mom take care of business. But you've fucked that up, and now the question is how bad you want it to come back and bite you. *And* her."

"You bastard." But the longer she stood there, the more the energy slumped out of her snarl, and finally she retreated into the room, shoulders falling. I followed and shut the door behind me. With the click of the latch, I saw her swallow thickly and half-turn toward the bed, only to stop herself and close her eyes before it entered her view.

"Give me a second," she said, hands up and shaking a little. A deep breath moved her chest and her breasts, where I caught the only sign that she was faking this: she had no bra on, and the firm little peaks of her nipples clearly said the act was turning her on – it certainly wasn't cold enough in the room to make them poke out like that. Still trembling, her hands went briefly up to shield her face and then dropped to her sides. Her eyes opened but stayed tight.

"All right," she said, glaring at me. "What am I supposed to do?"

"Well first," I said as I took hold of my belt buckle to unfasten it, "you're going to get those shorts down and drop to all fours so I can give it to you as quick and nasty as I can."

She didn't move, so I continued, lowering my pants and heel-toeing out of my shoes. "After that, we're going to cuddle up naked in the bed until I've recovered enough to give you a nice, long, slow, proper fucking that we can take our time at."

Doubt and calculation mixed on her face.

"My mom's going to be back before you could get through all that."

"What highway do you usually take out of town? And get those shorts off like I said."

"Uh ..." Her hands fluttered to the button of her daisy-dukes. "Seventy-five."

"Well, after the first round you can call her and tell her you took thirty-five this time instead, and she'll have to double back and waste another hour. Do I need to come over and rip those off of you?"

"Fuck, just – God."

She undid the button with a fierce twist and yanked the shorts down. Plain cotton panties stood out powder blue against her skin instead of the lacy things she usually wore for me if she had on underwear at all.

"Nice," I said. "Now turn around and drop those too."

Hesitantly getting her thumbs into the waistband, she turned halfway, then stopped. "Wait a second. Do you have a condom? No, what am I saying. She's gotta have a drawer-full of them in here somewhere, right?"

My mouth opened but stuck that way. "Uh ..."

Is she really going to make me put on a rubber? Or am I supposed to argue her out of it?

Gloria looked around her room as if it were a distasteful mystery to her. "Don't bullshit me. Where are they?"

"We don't use them," I said, "But she –"

Her head jerked my way and fixed me in a glare. "That's crap. There's no way my mom fucks you assholes bareback.

She's not a moron."

"No, she's not." I pointed across the room. "What I was trying to say was, she keeps a bin of them in the top of that dresser. Or that's where she kept them back when we still used them."

She walked immediately to the chest-of-drawers – an angry teenager walk, not a sexy Gloria walk. But her ass still moved beautifully in those shorts as she went, and her bare legs still looked fantastic beneath them.

Opening the drawer, she immediately found the condom stash and grabbed one out. "I said not to bullshit me. You're not getting out of wearing one of these just because my mom's not here and you think I'm some kind of dumb young college girl."

Wow, she's really going to push this, isn't she?

I held up my hands. "Seriously. When I hit ten years, your mom said she has a thing where, if you've been seeing her long enough and she really, *really* trusts you, and you're single and you don't play the town, you can skip the condom. You just have to promise that you don't have anything, and that you'll tell her if you screw anyone else, even using protection, and go back to rubbers for a couple of months until you can be sure you're testing clean."

She looked dubiously from me to the dimpled square package in her hand, then back again.

"Isn't that ... unprofessional? I mean, all those other guys must assume she's using safe sex with everybody, not just them. And aren't you worried one of the other ten-year club guys will lie to her and you'll both end up with something?"

I shrugged, adoring the baffled expression she gave me, like she had no idea how this worked or that we'd talked about it all before. Although I also wondered why she was getting so deep in these weeds. *Maybe she thinks the girl really wouldn't let it go.*

"I'm a fatalist," I said. "If I catch something, I catch something. A meteor could hit me tomorrow. And besides, she's worth the risk."

She put her fingers in her ears. "Don't go there. I do *not* need you telling me how good my mom's pussy is."

"Not how good she is," I said, stepping closer. "How good it is that she trusts me."

We had our eyes locked, and I was totally out of character now, at least in my tone of voice and the way I looked at her. For a moment, I thought I could see her fighting back a smile.

Then she wrestled it down and hardened her glare and, with a toss of the condom toward me, said, "Well I don't. You want to put it in me, you're going to put that on."

I shook my head, marveling. *I guess she's set on playing this real.* Not only did I not mind the condom, I actually got hotter knowing that if it *had* been Gloria's daughter there with me, she certainly would have demanded the same thing.

When I dropped my boxers, the fierce pole of my cock jutted out straight at her.

"Holy ..." she said, looking shocked and then looking angry at herself.

"What?" I asked, tearing open the condom. "It's not that big."

"Never mind," she said. "Just get the rubber on so we can get this over with."

"Oh, no," I said, getting back into my peeved-customer act. "I want to hear it. That's part of what you get paid for, saying nice things about your john's equipment."

She frowned. "I just ... it looks nice. It's a really good-looking one. And I thought, I guess I understand her not wanting it hidden in a rubber."

I laughed. "Gloria's a lot better at talking it up than that, but I guess it'll do." I waved the disk of the condom. "So do you like it enough for me to skip this?"

"No way," she said, steeling her face up. "I still don't trust you, and I wish she didn't either. And I hope to god there aren't very many of you in that club of hers. In fact ..."

She paused, and I couldn't tell if she was feigning hesitation, or fascination at the sight of me rolling the condom along the length of my shaft.

"Yeah?"

Her eyes rose from my crotch.

"Nothing. I just – well, there can't be very many of you. Can there?"

What exactly is she saying? Could I dig in, right now, and find out just how many guys she lets do her that way? If there was one thing Gloria knew how to do, it was find exactly the right tease to fan my flames. And the idea of being special to her fanned them very, very hot. What if there were just three of us, or two?

What if I was the only one?

"I've never asked her," I said, taking another step forward. "I wouldn't ever ask her, either. Because I think she'd tell me, and I'm not sure I want to know. But I do know that I want *you* to turn around, take those panties off, and get down on your hands and knees."

"Uh-huh," she said. "I *thought* that's the kind of guy you are."

She turned, put her fingers inside the elastic of her underwear. Her head went down and her shoulders scrunched up. Then she wiggled her hips like it was uncomfortable and lowered her panties in a series of halting jerks. When the waistband got low enough, I saw a tiny heart drawn on her right ass-cheek, I guess with a black sharpie for the outline and a red one for the fill.

Jesus, she thinks of everything.

"Nice tattoo. Your mom know you have that?"

"I'm an adult," she growled, dropping to one knee and then the other, fists clenching as she went. "It's my body, and I can do whatever I want with it."

"Mmm," I said. "Well how about right now we do whatever *I* want with it."

"Fuck you."

I resisted the cliché of saying that was exactly what I meant. She bent over, hands to the floor, the movement rotating her pelvis to bring that smooth, clean-shaven pussy into view.

"Oh, yeah," I said, stepping in close, kneeling down. "Wow, does that look fine. This is going to be so good."

She breathed sharply in as I put my hands to her waist. I could see her shoulders trembling. The latex of the condom gleamed tight around my dick, especially the bulbous head, pointed right for her precious entry. That sight had gotten so normal over the first ten years, but it seemed strange now – rare. *Like my cock's a Hollywood movie star dressed up on his way down the red carpet.* The thought made me wonder what kind of red carpet Gloria's daughter might have shown me, if this had really been her kneeling before me instead of her mother, who'd been shaved ever since I met her.

Sliding my hands from Gloria's waist to her sweet, lush ass, I kneaded the flesh there, one side at a time, with my right hand framing that false tattoo between thumb and forefinger. Meanwhile, centimeter-by-centimeter, I edged forward, rubber-clad dick swaying as it neared its destination. I let it bump up against one buttock, then readjusted so that the slack little cum reservoir at the tip tickled up into her butt crack.

She flinched very realistically.

Letting go of her bottom with my left hand, I took hold of myself and rubbed my barrier-protected penis head up and down her slit, where musky wetness gave another clue that she was faking all her reluctance. As I toyed with her there, bringing sudden intakes of breath with each nudge, feeling how easy it would be to plunge in and get started, I decided it was time to ask the question.

"So. What's your name?"

She was ready, no hesitation. "I'm not telling you my fucking name."

"No? What am I supposed to say when I'm about to come, then?"

"I don't care." Her voice steadied, became more determined. "Call me whatever you want. You're getting my pussy, you're not getting my name."

Damn. Well, it had been worth a try, even if I hadn't expected it to work. She'd been careful not to mention her daughter's name the whole twelve years I'd been seeing her.

"Okay," I said, rolling my cockhead around to just barely widen her pussy lips. "We'll go with Brandy, then. What do you think, is Brandy okay?"

"I don't c–"

With a lunge of my hips, I powered all the way in, smacking tight up against the curve of her ass in a heartbeat.

"Uff!" she said.

"Oh, damn, Brandy," I groaned. The first inch or so, there'd been almost no resistance. But then she'd realized what was happening and tensed everything up. The rest of the stroke was like plowing into true virgin territory. "Holy shit, you're so *tight*."

Through gritted teeth, she said, "That was rude, you goddamn asshole. You did that on purpose."

"Uh-huh," I admitted, taking hold of her waist again. "And I'm doing *this* on purpose too."

At a more measured pace, I drew most of the way out and gave her another stroke. Her cunt gripped me like extra-slim jeans on a plus-size model, squeezing so hard that if she'd been any drier, she would have pulled the condom right off of me, or maybe I would have broken through it on the in-stroke. This was not the usual vaginal calisthenics that she blew my mind with every week. This was her using pure willpower and muscle control to mimic the inexperienced hole of a woman twenty years younger.

"Good God," I said, slowly starting to fuck her for real. "You're not a virgin, are you?"

"Uhhh ... uhh, shit ... no, I've had boyfriends. Nggh, Jesus, I guess they were kind of small..."

"Mmm, yeah." I dialed things up, slapping it into her now. "You're liking that, aren't you Brandy?"

"No," she said, following it with a moan that said she was lying. "Just – nnh, you said you were going to make it quick – fuck..."

"Working on it," I gasped. *Holy crap, I'm going to have to get her to do this to me without the condom sometime. So fucking tight* ... "You could put ... a little ... action into it, if you want to ... make it quicker ..."

Her head shook, but she started moving her hips, just a little, in time with me. The added sensation rolled my eyes up in my head. "Oh wow."

I pushed harder, plunging in and out. Gloria kept her movements tiny, her whole body tense. It occurred to me that maintaining this sweet constriction for my dick might be taking her whole concentration, even wearing her out.

"Brandy, *uhh* ... this sweet ... juicy, college-girl ... snatch ..." I reached around for her tits, hanging free beneath her within the dangling fabric of her t-shirt. They fell into my hands, perfect and soft except where the nipples scraped my palms. I trapped each hard little nub between two fingers and rolled her breasts in circles while I thrust in and out, climbing higher and higher up the sensual slope toward climax.

Suddenly, she rared back against me. "Oh, FUCK! You're hitting my g-spot or something ... ahhh, God, what the hell *is* that?"

The tight purity of her grip on me melted into random tremors, rolling wild up and down the length of my shaft. Gloria tossed and swirled her hips, crying out, clawing at the carpet with her fingers. "*Uhh, uhh, fuck, yes,* fuck me!"

I held on and did my best to keep pumping, my brain mushy enough from the treatment I was getting that I actually thought, *Holy shit, how did this girl get so good so young?*

And then she was pounding on the floor with her fist and I was spouting cum up into her, inside the steadfast latex sheath of the condom.

"Fuck, *Brandy!*"

Oceans of semen roared up out of my balls, gushing through my cock. I could feel the rubber filling up, spunk intruding between its tight, stretchy sleeve and my pulsing shaft. Brandy – Gloria – held herself fiercely back against me as I clutched her, gasped, and spewed. Then, when the last expulsion twitched out of my rod, she fell forward, taking the loosened condom with her.

"Uhhhh..."

I sat back on my ass between her spread legs, listening to her moan and pant and watching my cum dribble down from the exposed ring of the condom.

When I got my breath back a little, I considered the angry-sounding edge in her groans and asked, "Mad at yourself for coming?"

"Shut up." Her ass clenched and shook. The spasm

squeezed more white fluid from the trapped rubber. "God. Damn."

Shifting and leaning forward, I lowered myself into place over her, keeping most of my weight on my elbows. She made no move to fight me. The limp damp length of my dick found and nestled itself in the crease of her bottom.

"Now," I whispered, mouth right by her ear, "imagine that instead of getting you there being a jerk and bossing you around, I'd done it kissing you, caressing you, being tender and touching you all the places you wanted, all the ways you wanted. Still think your mom's getting a bad deal and just being used?"

She shook a little beneath me. "I don't know. I still think you're a jerk. You were a jerk to make me do it, and you were a jerk the way you talked to me up until it, uh, started to feel good."

I nuzzled her earlobe a little. "Did I really make you, Brandy?"

"What? Yeah, you blackmailed me and said my mom would pay for it if I didn't –"

"And you think your mom would have talked about me the way you said she talked about me, called me 'one of the good ones,' if I was the kind of guy who would follow through on that threat?"

"Maybe she doesn't really get what kind of guy you are."

"Maybe she doesn't," I said. "Or maybe you do, and you just don't want to admit it."

"What the hell is that supposed to mean?"

"It means you talked to me at the gas station, and then you deliberately set things up so you'd be able to confront me here, alone, where I could have barged in and done anything I wanted. But you weren't afraid of that happening. So either you believed your mom that I'm a nice guy, or you were perfectly willing to have a not-nice guy come here and push himself on you."

"Which you did."

"And which you didn't even ask me 'please' not to do. And honestly, I don't really think I'm that good an actor. Are you telling me you completely believed I meant all that stuff?"

She lay quiet for a moment. Then: "But if you thought I wanted it, why didn't you just ask me?"

"Because you didn't *want* me to ask you. You wanted me to be a dirty, nasty, woman-using prick, and you wanted to get a taste of that. You wanted to put yourself in a position to be used, to have all your opinions justified, and also to get a good, hard, filthy fucking. Tell me I'm wrong."

More silence. I kissed her shoulder.

"So the question is, does either one of us *really* want to have you call your mom and stretch her wild goose chase out longer, just so we can have some fun together in bed?"

"No," she said. "Christ, it was so wrong of me to lie to her in the first place. You must think I'm a real shit of a daughter."

Lifting up, I said, "Roll over."

She did, and I settled back onto her, face to face, looking her right in the eyes.

"I think you're a smart young woman who cares about her mom but who has the same problem most young people have. You want to know better than your parents. I think that's completely normal, and the thing that's unusual about you is that you're challenging her for her own good, when most kids your age would be challenging her out of selfishness."

Quietly, with her eyes shining just a little wetly, she asked, "Is that really what you think?"

"It's what I thought when we were talking at the gas

station, and it's what I think now."

The ghost of an out-of-character smile crossed her face, and she brought her hands up, sliding across my shoulders, up my neck, into my hair.

"You really are nice, aren't you?"

"Isn't that what your mom told you?"

"What she told me ..." She paused, eyes flickering with hesitation, then settling into a decision. "What she told me was that you're her favorite. Her very favorite, ever."

I shivered at that. The cynic in me should have doubted it, should have at least considered that maybe she told a lot of her customers that. But looking down at her, I just couldn't. I had no choice but to believe.

"I –" Something caught in my throat, made me swallow. "Thanks. It means a lot to me, that you'd let me in on that. I mean, I've gotten the impression I'm pretty high up on her client list, but I didn't think" *I didn't want to hope* "I was at the top of it."

She smiled, opened her mouth, closed it again.

"What?"

"Nothing," she said, shaking her head. Then she scraped her fingertips down my spine. "You should get up, let me up. One of us should call her. And we both ought to clean up before she gets home. She's going to be pissed that I faked her out, and you're going to need to be extra nice to her to calm her down. I can't imagine what it will be like if she gets a whiff of our fuck smell on you."

"Hiding things from her isn't how I work."

"Yeah, well shoving things in her face *is* how I usually work, but in this case I really don't want to. I want to apologize to her as soon as she gets back, and I want you to make her feel ... the way you're making me feel, right now. Like you care."

I smiled and pushed myself up, stood. "That part will be

easy."

Wincing and wrinkling up her nose, Gloria tugged out the used condom and got to her feet, holding it thumb-and-forefinger like it was a dead rat. "Shit, you spew like a horse."

"Only when I'm having sex with the best."

We both laughed, and she walked over to the door into the house. Turned the knob. Pulled it open. Halfway out, she turned and looked at me – her lips had clamped together in a thin line. Then they loosened, blood rushing in and filling them pink.

"Dennis?"

"Yeah, what?"

A deep breath moved her breasts high, then eased out.

"She didn't say 'on her client list.'"

"What?" I didn't quite get it. Or maybe I got it and couldn't quite believe she'd said it.

"When she told me you were her favorite. She didn't say 'client.'"

Then she held my gaze just a beat longer, backed from the room and let the door fall shut between us.

* * *

Gloria's boudoir has its own tiny bathroom – a powder room really, toilet and sink and a hanging ring for a hand towel by the light switch. I urinated there, used toilet paper to wipe a couple of stray drops from the porcelain rim, then washed my hands and splashed cold water on my face to rinse off most of the sweat. I looked around wishing there was a washcloth to dab the rest of me a little cleaner with, but there wasn't, so I went back out and stood at the foot of the bed with the ceiling fan on, turning and air-drying the rest of my perspiration in the downdraft. By the time I'd mostly finished, the door opened and Gloria came back in, her face cleansed bare of makeup.

I stepped toward her, and she hurried to meet me, but just as I caught her up in my arms, she said, "I went too far, and before anything else, I've got to clear that up."

That made my stomach sink a foot or two.

"Um," I said, taking a wishful stab, "too far playing the bitchy daughter?"

She laughed and tip-toe kissed my cheek. "God no. That was so much fun, and such a ... *release.*"

I nodded and tried to smile back, head hanging a little lower than I would have liked. "Well, it's okay. You don't have to tell me what you did and didn't mean. It was wonderful, and I've got plenty of practice separating our games from reality."

She looked up at my hairline, lifted a hand to smooth it into what I assume was more presentable shape. It felt so right, her doing that while standing in my arms, breasts warmly cushioning my chest, face looking so at ease, even as it showed the mind behind it searching for the next words to say.

Maybe she did *go to far,* I thought, *make me feel a little too special. But it was great, and it was worth it, and this moment now is more than worth it too.* Somehow the self-pep-talk didn't quite convince me, though. Those last few words before she'd left the room ...

"Denny," she said, bringing her hands to my cheeks.

"Yes?"

"I didn't mean I went too far play-acting for the game." She took a couple of breaths, just looking at me. "I meant I went too far opening up. She's got three more years of school for me to pay for, and then there's another year more on the mortgage and on ... another big long-term debt. What I am right now is what I have to be for that long. I can't be anything else for anybody else, except my daughter, or I'll crumple and it will all fall apart and I won't be able to stand myself." Her fingers spread out across my chest. "And that means who we are right now is who we have to be for a while. Even if one or both of us wish it could be different."

I tried to come up with a reply. But I could barely breathe, much less think.

"So ... can you pretend that all I did just now was fuck you like my daughter would have fucked you? Can you keep going on being my very good customer and letting me be your paid woman?" Her eyes were tearing up now. "Because there's no way to take back the things I said, and I'm not going to lie and tell you I was pretending. But those words just can't be out there right now. I can't even – I can't know how you would even respond to them. Okay? Can we bottle them up, and just stick to being a whore and her trick?"

"No," I said, taking her by the shoulders and staring down at her. "For two reasons. One, I don't like that word. You can be my paid woman, but you can't be my whore. And two, you can't *just* be my paid woman, and I can't just be your very good customer, because you're already my very good friend, and that was before anything you said while you were pretending to be Brandy. Or whatever her real name is. The least I'll take is you being my exclusive provider of sexual services, with whom I am also on the most wonderfully friendly terms. And if that friend wants me to pretend I didn't hear something, I'll do it. Is that close enough?"

"Yes." She pulled herself tight to me and put her head against my chest. I felt a tear trickle down where her cheek met my skin. "Yes, that's perfect. Thank you so much, Denny."

"You're welcome," I said, squeezing her in return and working very consciously not to crush her. Then I let go with one arm and used a finger to tip her chin up so she'd look at me. "Now, if you don't mind, I think I've got at least an hour left on the clock, and I intend on fucking the shit out of you until your closing bell rings."

Laughing, eyes full of fire and relief, she jumped up so that I had to catch her under the thighs. Our lips met, our eyes closed, and in short order, we took each other to bed.

CHAPTER TWO

Summer carried on and disappeared. If Gloria had any trouble replacing Harry the Guy With the Belt, she didn't tell me. But either she'd figured out a way to make up the income, or she'd simply decided not to worry about it, because she glowed brighter every time we saw each other. One Monday evening in late September, as I lay in bed with her, sheets pulled up to our waists, I gave in to temptation and let myself inch toward the forbidden subject.

"You seem a lot happier lately."

Her fingers tickled idly at my chest, still damp from our exertions of a few minutes before.

"Well I would be, wouldn't I?" she asked. "With the Morality Patrol gone back to school."

"You've stopped smoking again, too. Or at least on days when I'm going to show up."

Shifting a little, she teased one of my nipples with her teeth.

"Totally your perversion's fault, mister."

"Oh? How so?"

"I can't smoke if I'm going to play 'Brandy' for you. She

hates cigarettes." Her face came back up next to mine, close enough to see the blush I felt rising through my cheeks.

"I haven't asked you *that* many times." But it was true that the only role-playing we'd gotten up to lately involved her pretending to be her daughter. "And anyway, I never insisted on perfect realism."

Her leg, bare and soft and smooth, slid up mine, bringing the knee across my thigh, then onto my other thigh, and then higher still until her crotch snugged up against my hip and her leg completely spanned my groin.

"I guess I'm just too much of a professional," she said, her tone thick like the heat of a summer day after rain. "If I don't force myself to keep up my standards, who will?"

"Hmm." The caress of her inner thigh across my cock brought a predictable response, even though our first screw of the evening had finished up just a few minutes before. "That doesn't feel like what you're trying to keep up is standards."

She laughed and ground her vulva against me, giving the flesh over my hip a moist kiss with it. "Should I dial things back and let us keep talking for a bit?"

"How about if you dial it up and let us keep talking until things get too hot and heavy for conversation."

"I like that." Working her hips, she used her leg's soft inner surface to encourage my hard-on while simultaneously wetting my upper thigh with slick strokes of her bare, aroused pussy. One index finger moved in circles around my right nipple. "What are we going to talk about while I'm dialing?"

"You still haven't told me why you've been in so much better a mood the last few weeks."

"Well then obviously –" She rolled up onto me, lowering the leg from my crotch to give her hand access, sliding her knee down between mine, and settling her steamy pubic juncture firmly against my thigh. Her chest came diagonally up across me, her left hand grasping and stroking my erection, right hand sneaking in between my neck and the pillow. "– that's because I don't *want* to tell you."

I pretended to pout, but it turned into a tremor and an "ooh," instead as she swiveled her grip about my shaft and began damply humping my leg.

"Is it a, uh ... is it a ... nh, oh ... nice ... what was I saying?"

She scraped my chin with her teeth, licked along my jaw, whispered into my ear. "You were about to ask if it was a secret. And yes, it is."

Damn, she's good. My brain was thinking it about her brain, my cock was thinking it about her hand, and my leg was thinking it about the dripping wet slit gliding up and down my thigh.

"How'd you know that's what I was about to ask?"

Her blue eyes bored into mine as her palm swirled the knob of my penis, squeezing out a bead of thick, lubricating fluid.

"Because we both know you've been tiptoeing around asking it for the last several Mondays, and we both know you're a bad boy for doing it, no matter how sweetly and innocently you finally managed to put it." Her smile kept me from being too speared by that. She was right. All summer, ever since she'd slipped and said more than she should have, I watched the stress leave her face, the light brighten in her eyes, the strength fill up her laugh. And all summer I had wanted to say something about it, and all summer I had felt her feeling me wanting to say something.

"Sorry. I know it's off-limits to – well, just sorry. I couldn't help myself. You're always beautiful, but it's just been shining through lately. How am I supposed to keep my mouth shut about that?"

Her smile deepened and she kissed me lightly. "All you have to do is say it so it's not a question. Just say, 'It's nice to see you so happy.'"

The caress and stroke of her hand continued, but had a hard time competing with that smile and the look in those eyes.

"It's nice to see you so happy, Gloria. Really nice."

"See how easy that was? Now say, 'You know what else would be nice?'"

"You know what else would be nice?"

Her eyebrows rose inquisitively. Her hand gave a couple of firm, questioning jerks on my cock. "No, I have no idea. Why don't you tell me something?"

Vixen, I thought. *Okay, then.*

"What else would be nice would be for you to sit on my face and suck a giant load of cum from my cock while I kiss you between your legs until you scream."

She laughed. "But I thought we were supposed to be talking until things heated up too much. And –" Her hips worked more forcefully. "– your thigh and I are having so much fun."

"Like I don't know you well enough to know you can talk around a hard-on," I said, pushing up with my leg to meet her. "And I can certainly talk between licks."

"Mmm," she said, grinding down closer to my knee. "But your voice will get all ... muffled."

"*Boo.* Puns like that aren't going to make me want to leave your mouth empty."

"Doesn't matter if it's empty." She crawled farther down until her pussy slid up and off my knee and her face neared my groin. "Like you said, I have lots of practice talking with things in my mouth. It's a good way for a person to improve her diction."

"Oh God, you're brutal," I said. "Please go down on me before I lose this erection from the pain. And swap ends so I can deal with some lips that aren't so smart-alecky."

"Okay," she said, grinning and then giving the underside of my glans a lollipop lick. "You've convinced me ... slick talker."

I groaned – then groaned again as she took me quickly all the way into her throat. "Oh, fuck, Gloria."

"Ngud, hmm?" she said around my shaft, eyebrows up and deep blue irises gleaming up at me.

"*Very* good," I breathed. "Come on, get your tail end up here before you make me forget I want to eat you out while you're doing that."

Her hands roamed up my belly and spread across my chest as she suckled root-deep on my cock. Then she curled her fingers and drew all ten fingertips claw-like back toward her, leaving tracks of electrified skin behind them as they went. Rising to hands and knees, but keeping her face firmly down in place, she swung around and deftly straddled my head. The smooth curves and valleys of her pudenda settled to my lips – engorged clitoris nestled in the upper mons, dainty inner labia bordering the dampness of her slit. Our earlier fuck had left her smelling of sex and sweat.

"Mmmgnn," she groaned around my cock as I feathered my tongue lightly around the hood of her clit and then latched on to give her a full, broad-tongued caress. Her lips retreated up my shaft, swirled back down, lifting and lowering at an increasing pace as I probed her labia and crease and finally sealed and sucked and licked to clean as much of the last fuck's leavings out as I could.

Her mouth popped loose from me and she sighed, "Denny ..." before diving back to the base of my shaft.

Sex with Gloria on top never fails to blow my mind, whether she's screwing me or blowing me, whether we're going sixty-nine or even if she's just giving me a hand-job. She has this ability to be fully in control, and yet also completely responsive, so that her search for pleasure never falters in its honesty, but never interferes with her doing just what my body begs her to do to please me. In this case, as she humped my mouth, the hungry rhythmic movements of her pelvis rolled up through her spine to accentuate the bobbing of her head and jaw. Whatever my tongue did to delight her cunt, she took and amplified a thousand times in her sloshing, blissful trips up and down the length of my cock.

"*Hhm, hhm, hhm* ..." she panted, tongue rolling down the surface of the dick that filled her mouth. Each whimper matched up to a forward-back tilt of her hips, surfing her clit across the tight-sucked circle of my lips.

"Yesss, Gloria," I said, with a kiss to her throbbing nub. "Yes ..."

The plan to carry on a simultaneous conversation disappeared pretty quickly. Her lips, their pressure and motion, the sweep of their firm, plush flesh up and down my shaft, disabled most of my conscious mind – and the part that wasn't absorbed in pleasure had plenty to do trying to return the favor. We made a humming, moaning circle of delight for a while without any more talk.

"Denny," she said, eventually, letting me loose just long enough to get the word out.

"Uh-huh?" I asked, doing the same with her pussy. For a minute, we both concentrated on mouthing one another's sex organs, and while we both made sounds, none of them came out remotely intelligible.

Then she raised her head. "I want to fuck you."

Her mouth bobbed back down, cheeks sucked tight

around my shaft, tongue writhing a serpentine course along the top of my cock. Up and down and up and down she maneuvered her perfect oral talents, each dip a gliding stroke of heaven. With difficulty, I kept my own tongue circling her clit, swiping across it every few turns like crossing a "t," trying futilely to keep up with her.

At last I gasped out, "Are you close?"

"Mm-hm." *Suck. Suck. Suck.* "I had a little one already." *Swirrrllll.* "Oh god, your tongue ..." *Slurp, gulp.* "I just want to ride you for a minute before I hit the big one."

"Uhhh," I groaned as she kept at it. "So close ... I think I'll blow if you sit on me." Kiss, lick, tongue-fuck. "Shit, so good, I don't know what to do ..."

She lip-nibbled all the way up and off my rod. *"That,"* she said as I drew her swollen bulb in through my lips. Her hand gripped the base of my cock as her spit air-dried on it. "That, about three more times ..."

Once, twice, thrice I did as she asked.

"Oh *fuck*, Denny –" She rolled off my face and in almost a single motion swept her hips around, straddled me, and enveloped the full length of my erection in her hungry, wet vagina. Grinding us together at our pubic arches, she threw her head back. *"OOHHHHHH-HUAAAAHH!!!"*

Caught in the wonder of her trembling, orgasmic cunt – staring up at the beautiful tension of her throat, the full round sway of her breasts, and the utter bliss of her lovely, familiar face, I felt my floodgates start to open. It was an instant of perfection with no room for complaint that I was about to come up her vagina instead of down her throat like I'd asked. But in the split-second between the inevitability of climax and its actual start, Gloria exactly reversed the maneuver that had put me root-deep between her legs and got my cock all the way back into her throat.

She bottomed out with her lips just as I came.

Clutching at her ass, I grunted helplessly, bestially, and thrust my face up into the dripping crotch that hovered above me. A champagne-bottle fountain of cum burst out of me as if trying to reach the ceiling, captured by Gloria's esophagus instead. The muscles of her throat gulped around the crown of my erupting penis like they might draw every ounce of fluid from my body. Her clit trembled and throbbed between my lips. Both of us groaned over and over, pressing our bodies as hard together as they would go.

"Mmm-mmm ... mm-*hmmm*!"

She collapsed heavily onto me when the last twitch of my cock subsided, keeping it in her mouth even though she had to huff like a train through her nose to get enough breath. Her sweat rolled down my body and her musky sex-gloss coated my lips and chin. I was panting too hard to tell her how good it had been.

Eventually, she pulled her face away and turned herself much less gymnastically to snuggle in beside me.

"Whoosh," she said, her lips now just inches from my ear.

"Yeah." I let my eyes slip closed for a moment as her hand played across my chest.

"Denny?"

"Hmm?" The amount of effort it took to crack one eyelid told me I'd better open them both before I fell asleep. The look in Gloria's eyes made that more than worth it.

"Thank you for letting me be selfish and get you inside me there at the end. I was going to come either way, but it was incredibly better sitting on you."

"Ha. That wasn't exactly my worst experience ever at letting a woman have her way. And then you ended up giving me exactly what I wanted anyhow. It was a pretty happy detour."

She smiled. "I didn't think you'd complain, or I wouldn't have done it. But I'm grateful anyway. You're a blessing."

We held each other for a while then, eventually moving into that proposed conversation – what I'd been doing that week, how she'd been thinking of getting a cat. She remained nestled in the hollow between my left arm and torso. At some point my hand on that side found and fondled her breast casually. Not long after, her right hand did the same with my soft, contented dick. We kept talking, too, as she worked me into full arousal, as I gently rolled her onto her stomach, then eased into place and entered her from behind.

The sex stayed languid, peaceful and tender, never reaching a feverish enough pitch to interfere with our verbal back-and-forth. Neither of us came by the time the quarter-hour warning chime sounded.

"Want me to get you there really quick?" she asked.

I kissed her neck and pulled out, moved off to lie next to her again. "No, I think I'm good."

Rolling onto her side to face me, Gloria smiled and caressed my cheek.

"So," she asked, "Brandy next time?"

A suggestive shimmer in her voice almost made me come all by itself. I rose up onto my left elbow to look at her and try to figure her out. "Look, that sounds really good. But if her being back at school is helping lower your stress levels, I'd rather not remind you ..."

"Stop it. I wouldn't have brought it up if it was going to bother me." She sat up cross-legged, breasts pert and perfect, vagina on unselfconscious display. "Can I tell you something?"

51

"Sure."

"I think I get off on it as much as you do."

"Seriously?"

"Sure. When we do *this* –" She made a gesture that took in the whole bed and ended with her hand sliding down my abdomen to tickle my pubic hair. "– it doesn't feel naughty to me. I mean, it's if-the-neighbors-only-knew naughty, like everything about my job. But it's not oh-I'm-being-such-a-bad-girl naughty. I got past thrilling over 'this is so wrong' a long time ago. But when I'm being her for you, I get some of that back. And ... I get to say some of the things I wish I could tell certain other clients to their faces. Not you – I never think about you the way Brandy talks."

"Well that's a relief. You promise?"

She ran a finger across her sternum, through the sweet valley between her breasts, then repeated the motion the other direction to make an 'X.'

"Cross my heart."

"Okay, then Brandy next time it is."

With a grin, she said, "Good. Because I have some very wicked ideas about what she might do."

* * *

The next week was a skip week, so I didn't pull through the alley to Gloria's driveway until the week after. Knowing that she had something special planned for our "Brandy" session made the two weeks go even slower than usual, and not for the first time, I questioned the decision I'd made very early on to never go past three visits a month. I chose three as my limit very deliberately, because it would always force me to endure a gap somewhere in the month and prevent my time with Gloria from becoming a week-in, week-out routine.

But there were a lot of months when three just didn't feel like enough, and a lot of months when fourteen days felt like much too long in between

This time, it just about drove me crazy. *It's totally going to be worth it, though*, I kept telling myself. *Just like every time the wait makes you feel like this.*

And I was right. As I parked in front of her converted garage and turned off my car's ignition, I had that chest-squeezing, arm-tingling anticipation that you can only get from something marvelous and physical that you've waited much too long for. *Look at me, I'm practically shaking like it's junior year again and Carla Philbert is unzipping my fly for my first blowjob.*

At the door, after I knocked, I found myself waiting still longer. Gloria almost always answered her door very promptly – Brandy never did.

Finally, it swung open, and there she was, blinking and looking dazed in a long pink nightshirt that said "Princess" in vertical white letters down the right side of her chest and abdomen. No bra, hair pulled back in a ponytail, a pencil stuck behind one ear and glittery lip-gloss on the gaping round "O" of her mouth.

Then her features tightened into that furious essence of Brandy, fierce and tooth-gritting.

"What the fuck, now you're chasing me down at school?"

At school …?

Before I could puzzle it out, she grabbed me by the arm and pulled me through the doorway. "Goddamn it, don't just stand there, somebody's going to see you."

With me inside, she poked her head out and looked both ways, then stepped back and slammed the door. The moment gave me a chance to look around, and it was my turn to blink and gape.

The boudoir was gone.

She'd redone the whole place as a dorm room – posters on the walls, textbooks and folders and spirals stacked on every open surface, teen jeans and t-shirts leaking out onto the floor from an overstuffed laundry bin. The bamboo screen that normally hid her computer area had been taken down, the computer and video equipment were removed, and the surface of her desk now held a microwave, several fast-food cups, and more of the ubiquitous notebooks and college texts. Most astonishingly, two twin beds sat where the satin-sheeted king should have been, one primly topped with a Laura Ashley comforter, the other rumpled and unmade, heaped across half its surface with a fluffy duvet in a lime-green cover.

Holy shit, how much did all this stuff cost her? For a split second, I imagined her buying beds and decorations and textbooks to the tune of more money than I owed her for the session or even for the whole month. Then sense caught up with me. I'd never seen the rest of her house – the beds might have come from a guest room, the rest of the stuff from her daughter's closet. But she'd still done a hell of a lot of work remodeling for a two-hour appointment.

When I finally turned back to her, I thought I glimpsed and instant of happy pride in her eyes, though her facial expression stayed completely in character.

"What are you *doing* here? No, I know what you're doing here – how the hell did you find me?"

She stalked around me and grabbed up a pair of jeans from the floor, started tugging them on one leg at a time while standing. The position let her nightshirt neckline hang down where I could look right in at her dangling, delightful breasts, and the delay let me get my head in the game.

Working on my composure, I said, "I know a guy who knows a guy in the, ah, registrar's office." *Shit, does the registrar handle housing or just classes?* I'd lived off-campus all through college, not to mention the fact that it had been twenty years. "I said I was your long-lost uncle and I wanted to surprise you, and a little bit of money convinced him that I was trustworthy."

"That fucker is so fired," she said, sucking in her tummy and pulling the waist of the jeans tight to button them. "Wait, what the hell are you doing?"

I'd started unbuckling my own pants, and I didn't let her question stop me. "What's it look like I'm doing? I'm getting ready to fuck you. And you won't get my buddy's buddy fired, because that will end up spilling the beans on how your mom pays for this dorm room and your tuition."

"No," she said. But her hands froze at her zipper and didn't pull it up. "We're done. You agreed last time, that was enough. Our score was settled."

Kicking off my shoes and stepping out of the slacks, I started undoing the front of my dress shirt. "Yep. Changed my mind."

She crossed her arms, hiding her nipples but squeezing the full swell of her breasts within the thin pink fabric of that shirt. Her face grew frustrated and anxious. "No ... you can't just ..."

I sailed my shirt onto a bean-bag chair in one corner. "I can't, huh? You mean, I couldn't email the dean of students your mom's website information? Or I couldn't email your mom the video I snuck of us when I was doggy-styling you last time?"

"You videoed – god*damn*. Fuck you, though. You couldn't send her that because she'd cut you off."

"Maybe she would," I said, tugging my socks loose one after the other. "But maybe she wouldn't. Maybe you'd find out your mom needs my money more than she cares whether I screwed her daughter. Either way, you'd never be able to take the high ground with her in an argument again."

"You're such a piece of shit," she said. Steely defiance shored up her expression again. "I'm not doing this. I *can't* do this. I've got a roommate, for Christ's sake. She could come back any second."

I shrugged. "Well, I'm not getting my clothes back on until you've put out. So if you're really worried she might come back, you'd better stop playing around and get to work."

Her arms went down to her sides, fists clenching and unclenching as she stared at me. For a moment, her eyes flicked down to my crotch, where my cock strained in desperation to get out of my boxer-briefs. The sight put a curl of disgust in her upper lip. She squeezed her eyelids tight.

When she opened them again, they all but burned me.

"*Fine,*" she spat. "And I guess I don't even get to say this time's the last time, do I? You're just going to keep coming back and blackmailing me into being your whore."

"See? You're a smart girl. You're going to do great at college. Now come over here and pull my underwear down and wrap your pretty little mouth around my cock."

She didn't immediately move. "Did you at least bring condoms?"

"Of course I brought condoms. I'm a very thoughtful guy."

That made her growl, but she walked over and got down on her knees. I couldn't help thinking, *Holy fuck, this is amazing.*

For twelve years, Gloria had been giving me the most amazing sexual experiences of my life. Better than losing my virginity. Better than my wedding night. Better than the best make-up sex after any fight of my marriage, and certainly better than any of the one-night stands after the divorce. But the last few months had been like summiting Mount Everest. Something about the mental layers of this Brandy game sent me into the stratosphere. Or maybe *everything* about it did the trick: imagining myself with someone as lush and young as Gloria's daughter but with all Gloria's long-practiced skills; having the freedom to be as crass and demanding as I could ever want to be; knowing how much relish she took in her role; appreciating how fantastically she improvised this character who was so different from her; hearing all the subtle clues she put into her voice and posture that told me even though her character despised and loathed the person I was pretending to be, a part of her horny teenage persona enjoyed being fucked like crazy in circumstances she had no control over.

The look on her face as she tugged down my underwear was a perfect example. Her mouth kept hold of its frown as my cock sprang free to wave itself at her, inches from her nose. But the tight clench of her jaw loosened, and the angry furrow of her brow softened, and her eyes blinked and took on a hungry glow along with their fire of resentment.

She opened her mouth and leaned forward as though hesitant, pausing to lick her lower lip with a bright pink salivating swipe of tongue.

"You want it and you know it," I taunted quietly. It made her grimace and glare.

Then she closed her eyes and dove onto me as though having to force herself.

"Oh, yeah, Brandy, that's it," I said as she got her lips three-quarters of the way down my shaft. Brandy couldn't go all the way down like Gloria could – I always bumped the back of her throat before she got to my root, and sometimes she pretended to gag a little bit if I tried to go any farther. But the look of her sparkly lip-glossed mouth sliding up the veined cylinder of my cock somehow made up for the lack of deep-throating. "Suck that thing, you pretty little college slut."

She bobbed, leaving me glistening on every outward stroke and trapping me in a plush oral embrace with every inward one. The fury went out of her brow, and her eyelids fluttered without ever quite opening.

"Holy shit, that's so good." The serpentine rolling of her spine plunged that beautiful face into and away from my crotch, bathing my dick in pleasure with movements that swayed her whole body, not just her neck and head. "Don't tell me you don't love doing this."

Her eyebrows squeezed down again, and a rough noise of anger came out to mix with the sloshing liquid noises of the blowjob. She sped up, clamped her lips harder, as though suddenly intent on getting it over as quickly as possible.

"Yes! Great, keep going ..." Faster. And faster. "Oh yeah. I'm just ... going to say, though ... mm, good ... I can totally see your nipples through your ... *uuh* ... shirt. You might as well stop pretending, and go ahead, and, *nf*, finger yourself ..."

Her bobbing slowed. The hand she had at the base of my shaft loosened, tightened again, then loosened further and dropped away to help her other hand struggle with the button of her jeans. Then it was back, gripping me hard as her fingers dove into her panties. Within seconds, she was panting through her nose and moaning around my cock. The quality of the blowjob declined considerably, but I didn't care. The look of her getting herself off as she sucked me felt better than the actual sensations along the flesh of my dick.

"Mmm – mmm, *mmmm!*" she said, sliding spastically back and forth down my length. Her tongue writhed. Her finger and thumb constricted brilliantly around the base of my shaft, pulling up a hot, looming anticipation in the ducts and vesicles that led to my balls.

"Oh, god, yes, Brandy –" I groaned and got my fingers in the hair at the back of her head. "Yes, do it!"

The hand in her crotch moved as frantically as her mouth did along my dick. Tremors of pleasure crashed across her face, tightening her forehead and the corners of her eyes. With every sharp, rapidfire breath she took, a pulsating moan built deep in her chest. Her ecstasy and power pulled me with her toward orgasm.

"I'm so close," I gasped. "I'm going to come –"

Squealing around my cock, she thrust me all the way home into her throat, her entire frame bucking in climax.

I unloaded into her like a firehose.

"*Uhhhhh* fuuckkk, Gl– ah, ah, *Brandy!*"

Her hands went around my ass and clutched me to her, driving her nose into my pubic hair as I throbbed and spurted deep into her fantasy-teenage esophagus. And despite almost saying her real name, that's where I was in that instant – wedged to my pubes in her daughter's mouth, teen idols watching me come down her throat from their posters up on the walls.

And then with a choking gasp, she fell away backwards from me, before I'd even finished. A squirt of semen hit her right breast as she dropped to her ass on the ground. A couple more white globules tumbled exhaustedly to the floor between her legs.

"Fuck, Brandy."

With the last of my orgasm behind me, I lurched down beside her, grabbed her tight in my arms and covered her mouth in fierce kisses, tongue seeking hers and tasting the rich, lingering hint of my own semen on it. Her hands crawled up my back, and she returned the kiss with a passionate ambivalence, making little mewling sounds that might have been pleasure or might have been self-disgust.

We ended up making out on the floor for five or ten minutes before she got hold of herself and pushed me away.

"Your cum tastes like shit, by the way," she said, back to glaring.

"You could taste it? Seemed to me you finally got me all the way past your tongue – never did that before."

"You were still spooging on the way out. Lucky I didn't puke on you, but it was worth it to make you come faster and get it over with."

I considered saying something about the deep-throating not having anything to do with how quickly I came. And it *was* really quick. Gloria and I didn't usually even get to the sex in the first five, ten, twenty minutes of a session. With Brandy, I seemed to be in one opening or another and blowing my wad quicker than I could have drunk a cup of coffee. Try as I might, though, I couldn't come up with any way to taunt her for getting me off so quickly, and it wouldn't have been part of the game to give her a compliment.

When I said nothing, she got up with all her body language showing relief and added, "Saved you the cost of a condom, too."

I laughed. "What, you think making me blow my load toot sweet means this visit is over with? You've got to be kidding. I'm going to warm up in a couple of minutes and fuck you in every corner of this room."

She'd been pulling the pink nightshirt away from her front and looking in distaste at the dribble of ejaculate on her right tit. Now she let go and clenched her hands at her sides.

"What? No." Looking around the room with stupefaction, she shook her head vigorously. "I have a *roommate*. She's going to be back –"

"Yeah, yeah. What I'm seeing is one bed that's perfectly made and your bed that's a slop-heap. Which means your roomie's a neat freak and probably anal about her schedule, which means you probably know *exactly* when she's going to come back."

Her shoulders slumped.

"See?" Standing up, I turned and stooped to retrieve a ribbon of condoms from my pants pocket. "Let's start off in your bed and then get more creative once things are really going. With the shirt off, too. I want to see your tits naked."

"How did you know the messy bed was mine?" she asked accusingly, as if it offended her for me to know.

I pointed to the over-full laundry basket across the room. "I've seen you in one of those shirts before, and if you're willing to leave your clothes looking like a disaster area, you damn sure wouldn't make your bed like you were in the army or working in a five-star hotel."

The logic appeared to annoy her even more. She stripped off her pink nightshirt, stomped to the bed, the red cascade of her ponytail swinging, and threw herself shoulders-first to lean against the headboard, legs together and quickly tucked under the comforter, arms crossed to hide her breasts. I walked over, smiling, dangling the condom strip like a pendulum.

"Come on, Brandy," I said, putting a knee up onto the bed, sliding in next to her. "How many times have we done this? And you're still acting like I'm going to believe you don't want it?"

She refused to meet my gaze. "Fuck you."

"I'm getting to that." With a quick twist, I tore loose one of the condom packages, then reached across her to put the rest next to her cell phone on the nightstand. I made sure my chest brushed her shoulder as I leaned, but she continued her statue-like stare. Settling back, I reached a hand in to grasp her waist and nudge forward on it. "Scoot down. Get your head on the pillow."

She did, moving her gaze to the ceiling instead of the wall. I watched her, loving the surly, post-adolescent pout she put on, and also loving the amazing degree of thought and control she used to create this fantasy version of her daughter.

I ripped the condom package, rolled the contents onto my dick, which now wagged rigidly her direction from my crotch.

"You come every time I give it to you," I said, moving one foot over between her shins. Her legs tensed, then went limp. "You've bitched and moaned and called me every name you could think of..."

Getting into place above her, I brought my second foot in and used it to gently slide her ankle to the side until my knees would fit between hers and I could use them to delightfully spread her thighs. Then I eased down face-to-face, latex-clad dick bumping its root against her mons.

"But you've never cried or asked me please not to come back. You're a smart girl, too smart to keep trying the same thing over and over again if you want the results to be different."

She glared at me through slitted eyes.

I reached down between us to rub the head of my cock against her opening

"How about it? Do you want to try asking, 'Please don't fuck me. Pretty please?'"

With a sneer, she tipped her hips and thrust up, taking me half inside before I knew it. I gasped a little.

"If I asked that and you went ahead, you'd be raping me," she said, bringing her heels up behind me to pull us closer. "I'll play your trashy games with you way before I'd let you rape me."

I dropped my weight down. She was already rolling her spine, screwing the shit out of me.

"Goddamn it, Brandy," I said, not cooperating with her movements. "If you really think I'd rape you, that's a total erection-killer. Take that back."

"Ha!" She rocked harder beneath me, a triumphant, angry grin on her face. "I'm gonna fuck you so hard you won't be able to go limp, no matter what I say about rape. Called you every name I could think of, did I? Turns out I had a bigger gun in my pocket than you thought. Now *you're* not so happy getting fucked, and *I'm* the one in control."

I tried to stay in character, tried to think of something cutting to say back, but she was really fucking me like crazy.

"Ah ... god," I groaned helplessly, thrusting back against her, "that's so good ..."

"Uh-huh," she said, circling her hips so I swirled in and out of her flesh, "your raping prick doesn't care what you want, does it? It just loves it some teenage pussy."

"Glo-*Brandy* ..."

Her arms and legs gripped me tight as she put her whole body into working my cock. In and out her cunt gobbled and disgorged me, sweet and hot and tight and swimming with the liquid of her arousal.

"Too, *uih*, chicken ... to pretend you're a *real* bad guy, huh?"

I lunged and pounded, gritting my teeth at her sassing.

"You're just a giant chicken. A giant ... cock, uhhh ...

you cock ..."

With a moan, I opened my mouth to call out her name, whichever one my lips decided to form – my brain didn't have the control to choose.

And then the cell phone rang on the nightstand between the two beds.

And she reached over to answer it.

"What the –" The shock completely froze me, but Gloria kept humping away as she swiped the screen with her thumb and put the phone to her ear.

"Yeah? Ngf, *what?*"

A voice on the other end said something. I blinked a couple of times, then put a scowl on my face and slammed powerfully into her.

"ghh! Kind of ... in the middle of something ..."

Answering the phone? Really? You bitch! Gloria, you are so fucking brilliant!

"Seriously – hhhh – can't talk ... you know that guy I told you about?" She held the mic end out away from her mouth and grunted, bucking against me as I ploughed away. The phone kept speaking. "No, fff, uh, not the cute one, the asshole who ... yes, that one. Yeah, *hhuh*, I'm fucking him – right – *now.*"

She trembled and shook, face clenching in orgasm. Then a giddy glow of triumph relaxed her features and she laughed wickedly. "You want to talk to him?"

"What? No –" But she held the phone up to my face anyway.

"Say hello, Denny."

All I could manage was, "Oh god ..." which brought a "Holy shit!" from the other end of the line in a female voice. I was pretty sure it was Gloria's voice – she must have found an app that would let her record a message and play it back at a set time. But I only heard the two words before Brandy, cackling and moaning, lowered the phone back to her ear.

"Hanging up now – hahaha!" She thumbed the red button and dropped the smartphone back to the nightstand. "How do you like that, you big – chicken – fucker! Haha!"

"Oh my god, *fuck!*" I shoved deep and came, so hard and so long I could barely believe it. "Uh! Jesus, damn!" Blurt and splash after spurting throb Niagara-ed out of me. I was caught in a spine-stiffening orgasm the likes of which my blood-deprived brain certainly couldn't remember at that moment. "Mmf, honey, so fucking good ..."

Gloria wrapped her arms around me and ground us together as tight as she could, her body still quivering and taut. "*UH!* Fuck, yes!"

Then, just like that, we were done, and she twisted and pushed and said, "Okay, get *off,*" and I rolled and she scooted and we ended up side-by-side on our backs, squashed together in the narrow twin bed looking up at the ceiling fan (which I thought spoiled the dorm-room facade a little, but after that orgasm, I really didn't care).

We panted for a little while. I resisted the urge to take her hand in mine.

"Okay, look," she said when she had her breath at least partly back. I turned my head. She got on her side, up on one elbow, to glower at me. "No more of that shit where you try to get me to admit something, right?"

"Ow," I said at the jab of her finger into my sternum. "What's that supposed to mean?"

"It means you're a dirty old man taking advantage of a teenage girl, and if I get worked up by the action and come, it's all from stress and physical stimulation. You've got my mom fooled into thinking you're a nice guy, but when you're with me, you're proving you're not."

"How so?"

Her eyes rolled. "Really? You're going to ask me that? I mean, you supposedly like my mom so much, but here you are cheating on her with me."

Apparently, the blood had still not fully returned to my head, because I found myself getting confused about what was play and what was real, how I felt about her and what I should say to keep the game going.

"Well, uh ... it's not ... really ... *cheating*. We're not exactly in a committed relationship."

"Sure you are. You're in her no-condom club, remember? Supposed to tell her if you fuck anybody else, and then use rubbers long enough to make sure you're clean. Have you told her about screwing me?"

I opened my mouth, but nothing came out.

"I didn't think so," she went on, smoldering. "So you're a bad boy, and if you want to fool yourself into thinking I'm a bad girl, you just go ahead. But don't expect me to play along. I'll keep spreading my legs for you until I can figure out how to get rid of your sorry ass, but all the orgasms in the world won't get me to say I like it."

As the glow of sex faded, I found myself able to get my role-play footing back. "All the orgasms in the world, huh? That sounds like a challenge to me."

"Hah. Dream on."

I rolled onto my side too, so that I could face her and reach around to swat her ass. "I don't have to dream. This piece of tail has me wide awake."

She looked down between us to see my cock stirring, still wrapped in its semen-swollen latex sheath. "Yeah. How did I know that was coming?"

"Must be learning something at college."

With a sigh, she rolled off the bed and stood. Even straight-shouldered and beautifully mimicking her daughter's haughty bearing, Gloria's body couldn't really be mistaken for a college girl's. Her modest breasts had held up to age okay, but certainly not with teenage pertness. The round swell of her belly and the kink of her waist showed too much maturity, her skin too many little telltale wrinkles. But somehow she had the energy and the fire. And while she was obviously no fresh-bodied teen, she still had a shape lots of women could only pray to Jenny Craig for. I could totally buy the package – which, technically, I guess I was doing.

Hands on hips, she said, "So what am I going to have to do to get you out of here?"

I kept my eyes on her while stretching for the condoms on the nightstand, which meant I had to fumble around a little before I found them. Every second watching her defiant, delicious form got me harder and harder. By the time my fingers landed on the strip of rubbers, I had a full-fledged boner again.

"I think," I said, peeling the used one from my erection, "that I want to fuck you on that pile of laundry."

With a flick of my wrist, I sent the little cum-filled balloon sailing across the room to plop right in the middle of the clothesbasket. Gloria's jaw slid open into a gape as a viscous runnel of my semen drooled out of the condom and down the front of a blouse, gooey white on soft powder-blue. Something genuine in her look of horror made me realize those were definitely her daughter's clothes, and that she'd expected to just hang or fold them back up after we were done. Then her mouth started to shape an astonished laugh, only to freeze and clamp down on the sound. Then something clicked and she was Brandy again.

"What. The. Fuck." She marched over to the basket, grabbed up the condom, scrunched it in her fist and then threw it at me. I ducked, and it splatted against the wall. Part of me felt bad about going too far, but another part of me spotted a playful flame in her blue eyes that said she was rolling with it and everything would be fine. She lifted the blouse from the clothes heap, staring at the pearly dribble that streaked its breast.

"What's the big deal?" I asked, taking a couple of casual steps toward her. "It was dirty anyway, right? Why don't you just suck the cum off, drop it back in the pile, and we can get to it."

This time, her dropped jaw was clearly deliberate, followed up immediately with a tooth-clenching scowl. "Oh, no. I'm not lapping up your spew *and* letting you ream me over my own dirty-clothes pile. You want me on that basket, *you* lick this thing clean."

"Me?" I asked, blinking.

She just thrust the jizz-spattered top toward me, spread across her hands.

I tried to figure out what the asshole version of me would do.

"What's the matter, scared of a little of your own man-juice? Haha, this is good – Mister Big Man's all squeamish about sucking up a couple drops of cum."

I took a half-step forward. She held the blouse farther out. Then, with a flare of inspiration in her eyes, she said, "Tell you what, you lick and suck it up, and I'll even pretend to like it while you're banging me on the laundry."

All by itself, the taunt in her tone put enough real humiliation into me to make me do what she said. Add in the layer of Gloria pretending to be Brandy pretending to enjoy getting fucked in a heap of dirty clothes, and I was moving before I knew it.

I grabbed the shirt from her and brought it up toward my face, meeting her I-dare-you gaze until it was almost to my mouth. Then I looked at the load of goo on the cloth and had a momentary shiver of distaste. It's not like I'd never tasted my own cum before, but this was cum that had been sitting in a lubricated condom for several minutes, and for some reason it was particularly unappealing.

A glance up showed a gleeful smirk on Brandy's face, so I screwed up my courage and stuck the slimy patch of cloth in my mouth to suck. Cold, salty-bitter goo slid off the blouse and across my tongue, with just enough hint of latex and chemical aftertaste to make it really nasty.

"That's it, work some spit into it and really get it clean!"

I tried to leer with my eyes while sloshing saliva through the weave of the fabric. Gloria just watched and laughed like a teenager reveling in superiority over all of adulthood.

"Blah. There." I tossed the blouse to her, a great dark stain of spit where the semen had been. "Clean enough?"

She put it to her nose, sniffed lightly, and shrugged. Dropping it back onto the basket-heap of clothing, she turned her ass to me, keeping her eyes on me over one shoulder. "Sure, mister cum-sucker. Now put one of those on and I'll hold up my end of the deal."

As I tore open another condom to obey her, Gloria knelt and got to her hands and knees across the laundry basket. She'd really piled it high, and the crest of the heap embraced her breasts and rib-cage as she nestled into it. Her ass, with that freshly marker-drawn heart tattoo, wiggled and rolled at me, flashing a bare, glistening slit and lovely mound.

"Come on, you spooge-drinking creep," she said, wallowing into the laundry, "get it in here and see if you're as good at getting a woman off as you are at slurping up your own jizz."

The insults only inflamed me more, and I quickly knelt

behind her, finished rolling on the condom, and got my tip aimed at her flush, swollen pussy lips.

"Oh, mister!" she said at the touch of my crown, voice an artificial octave high. "Is that your penis back there?"

I put one hand flat on the hard plane of her tailbone, guiding myself in with the other.

"Ooh!" she cried out in a mocking porn voice. "Oooh, it's so big and hard!"

The sarcasm dripped as thick as her pussy-juice did, both of them driving me crazy. I took her by the waist with both hands.

"Get ready for the fucking of your life, you little cunt," I said.

"Yes, yes, ooh, give it to me!"

I pulled half out and rammed in.

"Oh, it's like a baseball bat inside my poor teeny teen pussy! What a stud man you are – oof!"

The last sound wasn't entirely faked, as I smacked into her hard enough to scoot the whole laundry pile. Without giving her time to recover, I started fucking hard and fast. She kept her sweet, round bottom at a receptive angle, but didn't otherwise join in. Or rather, her hips didn't join in, but her vagina took me in with that incredible clench that she used to a mimic tight college co-ed fuck-hole.

"How's – *this*, Brandy?" I asked as I laid it into her.

"It's soooo good," she husked exaggeratedly. "Oh, gosh, mister, I'm coming already!"

She tipped her head back and forth, swinging her long red ponytail.

"Oh yes, I'm coming *so* hard from your, nff, your big stiff cock."

Still pumping fast, I leaned down onto her, digging my hands into the heap of her daughter's clothes. They felt soft and clean, at once beautiful and disappointing, because the fantasy of plowing into her atop a jumble of soiled laundry would have been that much better if they'd felt the part, if I could have dug up a handful and smelled the lingering girl-sweat and deodorant scent.

"Uh, yeah, Brandy. Uh, uh, you hot little cunt ..." My dick slid in and out of her as fast as I could thrust, and now she'd started pushing back in time with my plunging jabs. "Yes ... cunt ..."

"Yes, yes, it's so big in my tight little pussy!" The mocking edge faltered a moment as I drilled into her and made her gasp. "Ogh –"

Breathing hot into her ear, with a series of firm pumps, I said, "Yeah, you're starting to like that for real, aren't you?"

"Oh, yes, of course, you're such a stud with your giant, *auhh* ... penis ..." She'd started to quiver and pant now, and I kept working her as fiercely and steadily as I could. She rocked and twisted and shoved back in time. "Oh, oh, oh, your penis ..."

"Take it, Brandy," I gasped. "Yes, take it, girl ..."

Suddenly, she gave a deep and womanly groan. "*Ahhh, god, Denny!* Fuck me, fuck me ..."

Her head went down into the mounded clothes, muffling a scream of ecstasy.

"That's it – Brandy – you just *pretend*, just – like – that –"

Almost without warning, my orgasm boiled up out of me and exploded. Gloria's movements had gone spasmodic, uncontrolled. Her snatch quivered loosely around me as I throbbed cum out against the latex barrier of the rubber, filling it up with so many bursts I thought for sure I'd feel the blowback against my pubes before it ended. Wordless female pleasure squealed out through the laundry as I kept coming and she kept coming and the sweat poured off us both to drench the clothes beneath us.

When the last tremor of climax ran through my cock, I wrapped my arms around her and rolled us both off the basket onto our sides in the spill of clothing around it. We lay there panting, Gloria moaning softly, the blue blouse and a couple of other garments trapped against her breasts by my embrace. My erection softened and slipped out of her. Slowly we each got our breath back.

"Some, ah, really good acting there at the end, Brandy," I hushed into her ear.

"Shut up," she said, tightening her arms around mine.

I didn't argue with her, but rested, sated, flush against the naked curve of her back with nothing but our mutual sweat between us. Eventually a sigh went out of her and her arms relaxed.

"So," I said when I thought enough time had passed. "When's the next time you're going to be home to your mom's for a visit?"

She breathed in, then paused for a minute as if trying to decide whether to be nasty or just answer.

"Thanksgiving."

"Mmm," I said, nuzzling her ear. "Maybe I'll come over and give your juicy bird a good stuffing."

"No. No bird to stuff. My mom takes the holiday off, but she never cooks. We just sit around and argue or watch shit on cable."

"Really?" It surprised me to realize that I'd spent the last twelve years, whenever Thanksgiving rolled around, imagining Gloria the picture of loving motherhood baking up a traditional feast for her beautiful daughter.

She nestled against me. "My dad was a prick about Thanksgiving. Made her cook everything, and it all had to be perfect or he'd get pissed."

That's more than she's said about her husband in twelve years.

What kind of asshole treats a woman like this that way? Or goes off and leaves her?

"So now she hates Thanksgiving?"

"No, now she hates to cook it. I bitch at her about it because I haven't had a real Thanksgiving since I was nine, but she just tells me I should cook it then, and she'd be happy to eat it."

"So why don't you?"

She sighed. "I tried once, but I just ruined twenty bucks worth of turkey and burned the hell out of some rolls."

"Well did you ever try asking her nicely if she'd help you cook?"

A laugh snorted out of her. "Do I seem like the asking-for-help type to you?"

"I guess not," I said, squeezing her and kissing her cheek. "Let me have my arm back, okay? I need to get up and piss."

She raised herself up off the arm I had beneath her, and I disengaged and stood, stretching. Gloria rolled over and looked up at me.

"What time is it?"

I glanced at the clock on the nightstand. "It's – what? It's eight ten. Good god, was I fucking you so hard we missed the chime?"

"What chime?"

When I looked down, she had a perfect teenage what-the-hell-are-you-talking-about expression on her face. All about her lay her daughter's clothes, damp with the sweat of our sex.

"Your, uh, mother has a chime that goes off. To remind us time's almost up."

"Shit, that's a good idea. I'll set my phone next time. And it really gets rid of you?"

I grinned. "Hah, if you're really that anxious to get rid

of me, why are you already planning for 'next time?'"

That got me a glare. "I thought you needed to piss."

"I'm going," I said, turning toward the powder room.

Her voice brought my head around after a couple of steps. "Hey, Dennis?"

"Yeah?"

She was still flat on her back, head tilted to look at me upside-down. I couldn't read the expression. Then it went sharp again and she said, pointing, "Take your damn clothes in there and get dressed so you can get out of here, and I can go back to studying."

I walked back past her to my clothes strewn across the room.

"Sure, Brandy. Whatever you say."

* * *

By 11:00 a.m., when I pulled up in front of Gloria's house, I felt about ready to keel over from exhaustion. I'd been up since four that morning after a long, insomniac night, and I'd swear my heart rate climbed steadily with every hour past sunrise. The line at the restaurant might as well have been a cardiac stress-test. Traffic was light between the restaurant and Gloria's, but I still forced myself to drive slowly and with extra care, for fear that my jittery arms and hands would send me crashing off the road if someone honked or a squirrel ran in front of me.

It's just going to be a couple of minutes. Knock on the door, wait, say hi, hand over the food, she'll be surprised and say thank you, maybe we'll talk just a bit.

But of course I'd had over a month of should-I-or-shouldn't-I arguments with myself, along with daydreams of being invited in for a chat or to actually share dinner. And the inevitable fantasies of being invited to stay *after* dinner. So nothing I told myself did anything to calm me down.

Unbuckling my seatbelt with a shaky hand, I'd reached the point of hoping Brandy – or whatever her real name was – would open the door instead of Gloria. That would be quick. No chatting, no angst over whether she was about to ask me inside. Just a puzzled scowl and a handoff of the pre-made Thanksgiving dinner in its festively printed carry-carton.

She did make it sound like Thanksgiving was a lazing around day, I thought as I walked to the passenger side of the car. *It wouldn't be a surprise at all for her to make Brandy get the door. They're not expecting anybody.*

Or what if they were?

Popping open the passenger door, I looked up and down the street for any sign of approaching cars, but saw none. Just a chilly, breath-fogging Thanksgiving day along a quiet suburban street, some houses with extra cars parked in front, maybe – I couldn't tell because I never saw this side of the house. I had no idea how many parked cars would be normal here; my visits always took me in through the alleyway to her covered drive and finished-out garage.

Maybe I should have gone that way today, too. They could have somebody coming over – her friend Delia, or some of Brandy's friends. I'd heard a lot about Delia over the years, and I knew the daughter had made some very close friends in high school, the kind she'd really hated to leave when going off to college. If I bumped into some other visitor, would it end up causing awkward questions for Gloria? *"Who's this guy bringing you Thanksgiving dinner?" But no, she could always just say I was a massage client. They all buy into her massage therapy cover story. She seems pretty sure of that.*

But ... it would definitely be less intrusive to ring at the back. There'd be no doubt about which side of her life this unexpected visitor came from. And it wouldn't seem like I was presuming I'd be welcome, even briefly, at the doorway to the personal side instead of the business side.

Ultimately, though, if I wasn't really enough of a friend to make a happy surprise of dropping off holiday food, that meant I didn't really understand where Gloria and I stood. It probably meant I'd bought into some professionally applied white lies – that I had been kept more walled off from the real Gloria than I knew.

And if *that* was true, she might not even have Thanksgiving off.

So what made the decision for me was the horrifying specter of pulling through the alleyway and finding some other guy's car in her drive, maybe even seeing him come out straightening his tie and whistling. I *knew* that wouldn't happen. I *knew* Gloria really did think of me as a friend, if not even more than that. Someone special. She wouldn't lie to me about whether she worked the holidays. But paranoia just wouldn't let me have the confidence to test that certainty, and so I took the route that was maybe presumptuous and maybe risked me bumping into some other holiday visitor of hers. If that happened, it might be awkward, but it would work out okay. If the *other* happened – the guy in the driveway – I would be gut-punched.

As I made my way up the walk between her two tall elm trees, the front of the house said "ordinary family homestead" in a voice of reddish-orange brick and white trim. Charcoal shutters framed the windows, which showed only the slats of hanging blinds, and a finely polished door of dark wood stood centered behind the porch, an oval window with pebbly glass running from waist-high to hat-level.

I heaved myself up onto the stoop and stood there taking deep breaths, fingers clenched tight through the handle-holes of the restaurant box.

Okay. Just hit the doorbell and let things go from there.

With a little maneuvering, I lifted and turned the box until I could get a thumb out and press the round button for the bell. Just like always when you really want to know if a doorbell works, this one made no sound that carried out through the door, and I had to stand there fighting the urge to press it again.

After a minute, a figure moved up to the rough glass of the front-door window, rendered hazy by the texturing – but too tall to be Gloria.

The door opened.

Though I'd only seen her face twice, and she'd only seen mine the same number of times, I recognized her at once and saw that she caught up just a second or two later, her look changing from curious to suspicious as her dazzling blue eyes dropped from mine to the box and swung back up again.

"Why ..." She stopped herself, crinkled her pretty nose, then started again. "What are you doing here?"

I gave the box an explanatory heft. "Sorry, I'm not trying to butt-in on your holiday. Your mom mentioned she didn't cook Thanksgiving dinners, so I got this to drop off for the two of you. I thought you might like some traditional turkey and fixings for a change."

The suspicion turned to bafflement, then to discomfort, as if she realized I was just there to be nice but she didn't want to believe it.

Holding the box, and keeping my eyes off her tall, full figure in its sweater and jeans, I nodded back toward my car and said, "You can just take this and I'll –"

But the girl I thought of as Brandy whose name wasn't actually Brandy turned and shouted, "Mom, it's for you!" pushed the door to just a crack, said, "She'll be here in a second," and fled.

Gloria showed up a moment later in a shapeless grey sweatshirt and matching pants, and the look of unexpected wonder as she saw the big restaurant carton flooded me with happiness. Just the way her eyes widened banished the stress and jitters and anxiety and put a glow in me that I had done exactly the right thing. Looking up from the box, she stood tiptoe as high as she could, held my shoulders for balance, and leaned over the food to kiss me on the cheek.

Flush with pleasure and embarrassment, I said, "I just thought, you know, when you said you never cooked for Thanksgiving –"

"Of course," she said, settling back to her soles with a smile. "This is so you, Denny. You're lovely."

"Anyway," I shrugged the box upward, "I can hand this off or bring it in and set it down, and the two of you can –"

Gloria laughed and stepped aside, pushing the door wider as she got out of my way. "And that's so you too. Don't be ridiculous. You can't bring Thanksgiving dinner and not stay and share it."

From around a corner inside, not-Brandy said, "Mom!"

"Hush, honey." Something occurred to her then, and she looked back at me and said, "I mean, unless you've got somewhere else to be – I don't mean to assume ..."

"No," I admitted, "my friends Bob and Leisha invited me to their place, but I went last year and it was awful. Kids hollering, Bob's father-in-law giving me a day-by-day breakdown of all his stock trades for the last month, vegan turkey substitute ... no can do."

"Good. The kitchen's through there and around to the left."

Moving past her, I heard her shut the door behind me and found myself inside Gloria's house.

Light flooded in from the right side of the entryway –

the direction she'd pointed. A daisy-yellow living room opened up there, fireplace diagonally opposite me, couch with beaten-up upholstery facing the main wall to the right, where a mid-sized plasma TV sat atop an entertainment center. Gloria's daughter stood between the couch and coffee table with a book in her hand and a look of stymied frustration on her face. She stared at me as I took a couple of steps into the room, nearing the back of the couch.

"Denny, this is my daughter, Kaylee. Kaylee, this is Dennis."

"We've met," she said in a tone flatter than a frying pan.

"Yes, but that's not the same thing as being introduced," Gloria responded. "Don't be rude."

Not knowing what else to do, I said, "It's nice to meet you, Kaylee."

"Yeah. Sure." Her eyes went from my face to the boxed Thanksgiving feast, tracking it as I moved on toward the kitchen, which I now saw beyond a pass-through bar that separated it from the living room. An ambivalence in her expression said that no matter how aggravated it made her to have her mother's customer invade their home, she really had been a long time without a proper Thanksgiving meal, and couldn't help being lured by it.

I made my way around the corner into the kitchen, done all in white cabinetry with a round four-seat table in the breakfast nook. The house appeared twenty or thirty years old – clean and well maintained, but hardly the most stylish place I'd visited. On one side of the room, the range and oven looked like original equipment, while the stainless-steel refrigerator two cabinets down was clearly new. On the other side, the sink and dishwasher had obviously not been replaced since the house was built. It looked like a kitchen where things were allowed to stay until they broke, though kept clean and polished in the meantime.

The microwave from "Brandy's" dorm room sat on one faux-granite counter, next to the fridge.

"So ... where do you want this?"

Gloria had followed me in, a little farther back than arm's reach. She looked around at the counters and tables. "I don't know – what do we have to do to it?"

I looked down at the printing on the box, despite having already read it five times in the car.

"It says an hour of reheating time. I guess the turkey will have to go in the oven or something."

From the living room, Kaylee made an *ughh!* noise. I couldn't tell if it signified impatience at having to wait that long to eat or at having to tolerate my presence the whole time. But glancing through the bar, I noticed she'd sat back down on the couch with her book and her frown, when she could easily have dashed away to her room.

Gloria put a hand on my shoulder and pointed next to the sink. "Well, let's unpack it there and see what we're looking at."

The next hour may have been the happiest non-sex hour I'd had in fifteen years. I tried to offer to do the food prep myself so that she wouldn't have to cook, but she refused to hear of it, and from there we unloaded the carton and spread everything out and leaned side-by-side on the counter reading the instruction sheet together with her hand resting beautifully between my shoulder-blades. Once a game-plan came together of what to oven-heat and what to microwave and when, we got the turkey in the oven and found ourselves with nothing but time to wait. She pointed to a coffee-maker in one corner.

"Should I make a pot while we're waiting?"

"Sure, that sounds great."

Leaning to look through the bar, she asked her

daughter, "You want to come have coffee with us, Kaylee?"

"No thanks." A dismissive hand waved the offer away without even a glance up from her book. "Awkward enough already."

Gloria laughed and rummaged in a cabinet for a tin of coffee, a couple of mugs, and a sugar jar. "Go on and sit down," she said, tilting her chin toward the table. "This will just take a second."

What I really wanted was to step nearer, take gentle hold of her by the waist, and move with her as she got the coffee going, so that I could smell her hair and the scent of ground coffee beans and feel close to her and caught up in her life. But I didn't, and to tell the truth, watching her move about the kitchen from my place at her table felt almost as good.

"Okay," she said, leaving the coffee to percolate and coming to join me in the breakfast nook. "Sorry I don't have one of those Kurgig-whatevers that zaps the coffee out in two seconds. We're cheap and old-fashioned around here."

"I'm sure it's better than the crap that comes out of the machines at my work," I said, watching her slide into the chair adjacent to mine. Beautiful Gloria, her freckled face bare of makeup, eyes the blue of oceans seen from space, red hair a little tousled, as if she'd brushed it lazily this morning and taken no special care with it since.

"So how's your week been?" she asked, looking as though the subject actually interested her.

"Pretty quiet. Half the office took the week off. Last week was a bear, though, everybody frantic to get enough ahead of schedule that a week off won't blow any deadlines."

The coffee-maker gurgled. With a mischievous grin,

Gloria said, "That's the advantage of being in my line of work. When I take the week off, there's nothing to blow."

"MOM!"

Hearing Kaylee's squawk, the two of us broke up laughing. I tried to hold it in as best I could – I didn't want to give her any more reason to hate me, and I know teenagers can't stand to be snickered at by adults. But Gloria let loose without restraint, and hearing her, seeing the delight in her eyes, made it wickedly difficult to stifle my own laugh.

The coffee finished, was poured and stirred. We talked and sipped and caught up on the last week and a half. Holiday weeks were almost always skip weeks for me and Gloria, certainly if her daughter ... *Kaylee, so strange that it wasn't Brandy* ... was going to be at home. At some point, the surly teenager got up and went in to the refrigerator to get herself a soda, making the entire round-trip without ever casting her eyes our way, even though Gloria leaned in and whispered to me while she was walking toward the fridge.

"It's okay if you look at her ass. I won't be offended. She's got a hell of an ass, doesn't she?"

My face went bright red, or at least felt like it. I also just about choked on my coffee. I really thought I'd done a better job at hiding what my eyes wanted to do than that.

She sat back up as Kaylee returned around the corner of the bar, carrying her soda can to the couch. Then, when the book resumed its blocking duties in front of her daughter's face, she put her mouth near my ear and asked, under her breath, *"Do you wish I had an ass like that?"*

No, I thought, *because then I wouldn't get to see the ass you've got now, and I really like your ass. But ... partly yes, too, I guess. Kaylee's got a pretty awesome butt.*

"Let's, uh, talk about that later," was all I said, keeping

my voice quiet as I could. She grinned and tapped my foot with hers below the table. Then she looked over at the kitchen clock.

"Turkey's almost done. Time to start getting the sides heated up."

Everything came in its own microwavable or oven-safe container – gravy, mashed potatoes, corn on the cob, rolls. We got them into the appropriate cooking appliances, and then Gloria found the right serving dishes for everything. Soon we were loading it all piping hot onto the table.

"Lunch, Kaylee," Gloria said.

Her daughter got up and came into the breakfast nook, an uncomfortable, uncertain expression on her face. "Look, if it's okay, I'll just make myself a plate and take it to my room."

"No, it's not okay." Gloria's face and voice carried that firm, stern opposition parents can use with their children and nobody else can really match at all. "We have a guest, and he's gone out of his way to bring us this wonderful meal, and –"

"Yeah, because he ..." The reflexive teenage interruption trailed off. Her mouth clamped down frustratedly.

"Because he what, Kaylee? Because he wants to get into my pants? That's pretty obviously *not* the reason he came over, right?"

Silence. Gloria let her face soften.

"Kaylee ... please?"

With a grumbly expression but no further complaining, Kaylee moved over to the table and sat, taking the chair on the other side of Gloria from me. That put her as far as possible from my spot – but also meant we faced each other directly across the tabletop.

"Thank you, sweetheart," Gloria said, touching her daughter's hand.

"All right," I said. "I guess let's eat."

The meal went better than I would have expected, given Kaylee's starting attitude. I managed to ask her about her classes and get some grudging answers, and when I put a little effort into follow-up questions, she apparently decided to relent and let loose with actual details. She was taking some crazy stuff – advanced calculus and computer and engineering courses that I wouldn't have touched unless my major required it. But she hadn't even declared a major yet, and got a bit defensive about that when I asked.

Gloria had told me her daughter was smart. I'd assumed she was being truthful about that. Listening to Kaylee talk, though, and watching her vibrant blue eyes, made it clear to me that Gloria had exaggerated nothing. She had the passion and vivacious articulation that you only find in brilliant youths – people whose brains are so sharp they can capture and analyze the whole world, but whose experience is still too limited to understand that there are blind spots in every analysis and limits to the reach of the mind.

We kept talking a good half-hour after we'd all gotten full. I barely noticed the food as I ate, working so hard to keep Kaylee's sudden openness from snapping shut again – and also half-high on the glow of appreciation in Gloria's eyes as she watched me interact with her daughter. It helped a great deal, I'm sure, that Gloria had gotten a bottle of wine out along with all the serving platters, and the three of us had put away most of the alcohol over the course of the meal.

At some point, though, the conversation reached a lull, and the diversion of whatever subject Kaylee had been discussing wrapped up and left her, and she seemed to realize that she'd come perilously close to sitting comfortably at a table having lunch with her mother and one of her mother's johns.

Her mouth crimped a little, and she said, "Well, I'm bloated. I'm going to take my book and lie down in my room and —"

"Oh, no," Gloria interrupted. "Denny brought the food, he and I got it ready, and you're going to put everything away and do the cleaning up."

"Mo-omm ..." she whined. But the complaint only got her a commanding stare, so she rolled her eyes and stood up, sighing. "Oh all right."

"I'll help," I said, standing up as well.

"Nope," Gloria said. "You're going to go in the living room and strip down to your underwear, and I'm going to do something I've never done for you."

"AAH!" Kaylee shrieked, almost dropping the turkey platter she'd lifted off the table.

I'm certain I looked equally horrified. But Gloria just laughed at both of us.

"Get going, you two. I'll be back in a minute with my massage table."

Two people as different as Kaylee and I have probably never felt as identical a sense of relief as we did in that moment. When I looked at her, I saw her looking back, blue eyes full of *oh-my-god-can-you-believe-she-just-did-that-to-us?*

Then she straightened up and came around the table carrying the turkey, her composure returning enough to let her say, "I hate you, Mom."

I went into the living room and stood there awkwardly. Gloria had disappeared somewhere into the back of the house, where I presumed the bedrooms could be found. It looked like a folding massage table could be set up either just in front of the fireplace (*No way – Kaylee will have full view of that the whole time she's working on dishes*) or along the front wall, between the entryway and the hallway that led back where Gloria had gone. I moved to the second choice, and tried to get my courage up to pull off my sweater and start unbuttoning my shirt. But even from this angle, Kaylee would be able to see me stripping as she went back and forth from the table to the interior of the kitchen.

By the time Gloria returned, carrying her folding table by its handle, I'd managed to get out of my sweater and shoes but nothing else.

"Well this is the slowest I've ever seen you undress," she said, lifting an eyebrow.

"Oh, come on," I said, glancing toward the kitchen. Kaylee made another trip to the table, looked over at us.

"Ugh," she said, picking up a couple of dishes and hurrying away. From around the corner, she raised her voice to continue, "I'm almost done moving everything, and trust me, I don't want to look anyway."

Gloria pointed her eyes at my belt buckle and then down to the floor. "Let's go. I'll have this thing set up faster than you can say 'cranberry sauce.'"

"All right, all right." I worked at unbuttoning my shirt. True to her word, she flipped the table open, got its legs out and locked, and set it upright by the time I'd shucked the shirt and started on my pants. "T-shirt off too?"

"Up to you."

My eyes flicked toward the kitchen involuntarily. I couldn't see Kaylee. The table was bare. I left the t-shirt on anyway.

"Okay, so how do I ... ?"

"Just get on and lie on your tummy with your face in here," she said, patting the middle of the cushioned surface and then running her hand up to indicate the padded oval face-rest at one end.

Gracelessly, and with another embarrassed glance at the kitchen, I sat on the table's edge, lifted one foot and then the other, and rolled over onto my stomach, scooting and shifting until I had my face lined up with the head-rest's opening.

"See? Easy. Now close your eyes and relax."

Closing my eyes was easy. Relaxing, not so much ... at first.

Gloria's hands came down and rested perpendicular to my waist, side-by-side at the small of my back. "Come on, Denny. You can do better than that."

I took a deep breath and willed my muscles to un-tense.

"There you go." I could hear the smile in her voice as she said it. Then her hands started to move.

Very quickly, the remaining tension went out of my body and I found myself floating in darkness, as if the firm, gliding pressure of Gloria's fingers were my only connection to reality. She hummed lightly as she worked, but I couldn't identify any particular tune. Stress-knots and kinks in my sinews yielded before the power of her hands, bringing groans that I should have worried would be misinterpreted by Kaylee. But what Gloria was doing had me beyond worry. From my back, she moved up to my neck, then out across one trapezius and then the other, then around the shoulders and down each of my arms, then each of my legs. At some point, I realized that the noise of dishes and water in the kitchen sink had stopped – that Kaylee must have already finished and walked past us to her room. I found it didn't really make any difference to me.

Eventually, when I felt I was about to melt and drain away, Gloria patted one hand between my shoulder blades. "Roll over."

I did, taking care not to get too close to the edge, in case I fell off or unbalanced the table. Once I'd gotten on my back, she leaned over me, took one shoulder in each hand, and hooked her thumbs into my deltoid muscles right where the ends of my pecs joined up to them.

"Oh god." I'd opened my eyes when I turned over; now they rolled up into my head and had trouble focusing when they came back down. "Ohh."

Gloria smiled and continued circling her thumbs deep into my aching flesh, driving away cricks and pangs that I hadn't even known were there.

"Listen," she said, moving down along my right arm, "When I've wrapped this up, we can make some more coffee and sit and chat for a while, or watch some of the football game if you like. But I can't invite you to stay."

I nodded, watching her work. "Sure. That's not why I came."

"I just wanted to make sure you understood."

"Of course I understand. Kaylee would –"

"No." Her fingers paused, thumb at the lower end of my bicep. "Kaylee lives every day knowing her mom is a whore."

"Gloria ..."

"I know you don't like it, but it's the word she would use. It's what she thinks about what I do, and compared to that, having a man I like sleep over would be nothing." Shaking her head, she returned her gaze and her attention to my arm. "No, the reason I can't ask you to stay is, this is as far as I can go and still keep you as a client. I can accept a sweet Thanksgiving dinner as a gift from a customer. I can turn around and give you a massage as my own Thanksgiving gift back. But I can't take you to bed – to *my* bed – and still keep screwing you for money. I just can't. And what sucks most about that is, I really, really need you as a client. Not for the money, I could make that up somehow. But whenever I start doubting what I do, whenever Kaylee tries to insult me into quitting, I can think of you and I know she's a hundred percent wrong. Anytime

I'm thinking I have a shitty job and it makes me a shitty person, I can fix it. All I have to do is look at my Monday evening calendar."

I sat up and took hold of her forearm, putting my other hand on top of hers. "Gloria, you're the last person in the world who should think of herself as shitty."

With a smile, she extracted herself from my grasp and pushed gently at the center of my chest. "And that's exactly what I'm talking about. Lie down and take your massage."

I did, but I wasn't ready to let it go. "I thought you said you had lots of decent clients."

"I do," she said, pinching the meat between my thumb and palm with one hand, using the other to rub a thumb and forefinger slowly down each of my fingers in turn. "And lots of annoying ones to balance them out, and a couple of real buttholes to pull me down if I let them. But nobody can tip my balance the wrong way when you're on its happy side, Denny. And if I bring you over here past the boudoir door, I'm going to have a really, really hard time leaving this side of the house for that one every day."

We could work something out. I could ... What? Support her financially so she could quit? Support her emotionally so she could cope with her work even if I wasn't part of it anymore? Of the two of us, she knew what either one of those would take, and I had no idea.

"Okay," I said. Gloria finished with my hand and laid it back down. The whole arm felt like a limp noodle, in the best possible way. Walking around the head-end of the table, she began working on the other side. "But what if – just hypothetically, let's say – what if it reached the point where I decided I loved you, and told you so?"

She laughed. One hand left my bicep to pat me on the cheek. "You're so sweet. It wouldn't make the least bit of difference at all. Just like it wouldn't make any difference if

I told you I loved you. And don't pretend you don't know why it wouldn't make any difference. Let's just be happy with how things are right now, okay? Because they're good, aren't they?"

I was on fire to grab her and pull her down into my arms.

"Yeah, they're great."

She finished my massage and we watched part of the game from her couch, with me following her lead when she put her stocking feet up on the coffee table. We didn't sit close enough for me to put an arm around her, but once in a while her toe inside her sock touched mine inside mine.

And really, that was enough.

CHAPTER THREE

When the door opened and I saw Kaylee, I had a half-second of happy deja vu that sent me straight back to the first time I'd met her. But after that half-second, the look on her face dropped any pleasure out of my heart like a sink-hole.

"Kaylee ... What's – Jesus, has something happened?"

She nodded, biting her lower lip as if to hold some terrible secret in. Her shoulders trembled under the uncombed mess of her long red hair, and she had her arms wrapped tight around herself.

"Your mom –"

"She was in accident." The girl's voice came out raw and uneven.

Unable to help myself, I took hold of her by the arms – half to comfort her and half to squeeze something out of her that wouldn't be the worst possible news. She closed her eyes for a second, then said, "It's not that bad. Some cracked ribs and her leg's broken in three places. Last night."

The way she sniffled and shuddered every other word confused me, made it hard for my brain to click on what she meant. But ... *Gloria isn't dead or in a coma.* The utter relief of that kept my legs from folding under me and let me find the backbone to approach whatever had Kaylee in this state.

"Okay, so help me understand. Do you want to go inside to talk?"

She glanced behind her, into the boudoir. Her shoulders nudged upward, then slumped back down. "Sure."

I got her inside, guided her to the loveseat, shut the door. "Take some deep breaths and relax. I'm going to get you something to drink."

Head in her hand, eyes closed, Kaylee nodded. I kept talking on the way to her mother's microfridge and wine stash.

"So if Gloria's going to be all right, then what? Why are you so upset?"

"Dennis, her leg's broken in *three places*. She's not going to be able to work for two or three months." Her head came up off the hand, leaving her fingers tense and hooked. Her voice twisted upward in tone and volume. "We're going to lose everything. The house, the car – I won't be able to go back to school in the fall."

I poured her a big goblet of Gloria's burgundy and carried it back over. "Look, no, they don't foreclose on you after you miss a payment or two, and maybe I could loan you something to help with tuition ..."

The words were out before I could think about them and remember how completely tapped out I was at the moment. But it turned out not to matter. Kaylee's eyes looked into mine, her face distressed by my obvious ignorance.

"You don't get it. We're already two or three months behind on the mortgage from when mom lost a big ... client, last year." *Shit. Harry with the belt.* "She gets a little caught up and then falls back again. And what, are you totally loaded or something? Stanford's *expensive*. Sixty grand a year."

Stanford? Jesus, Gloria said she was smart, but I didn't know she meant that *smart.*

"Okay, well ..." *Fuck, that's five grand* a month. *And there's what, twelve hundred bucks in your account?* My savings had been completely shot that spring when my stepdad went off his antidepressants and decided to burn down the house with him and my mom in it. The fire department got them out, but the insurance called it arson and wouldn't pay, and on top of that they were underwater on their mortgage. I'd had to empty out my IRA and take the penalty to keep them from going homeless. "Are you already maxed out on student loans?"

She shook her head, eyes rolling. "No, no. You just don't ... Mom couldn't risk having her finances looked into by signing me up for loans or financial aid. She makes a crap-ton of money, somebody would start wondering how a massage therapist pulls in twenty grand a month."

I didn't count how many times I blinked before being able to reply. "How ... can she be behind ... if she makes –"

"Fuck, has she not told you this stuff? My dad owned his own company and he did something and got his ass sued off – like, millions of bucks in the hole. And then he went out drinking and drove his car off an embankment. And she'd let him put her on all the paperwork for the company, so she's on the hook for the judgment. Why else would she have ... she really never told you this shit?"

My head shook, dazedly. "She's not big on talking about her – your dad."

"Huh. Well, nobody could blame her for *that.*"

Standing there watching her as she took a big gulp of wine, I tried to figure out what I could do. Her eyes searched my face as if some tiny chance of a miracle might be hidden there, but she obviously didn't find it.

"Look," I said at last. "Why don't we go see her?"

Talking to Gloria can make anything better.

Kaylee, though, stopped her miracle-search and squeezed her red-rimmed eyes tight. Then she made a fist of her free hand, pressed it against her forehead, and reopened her eyes looking as grim and hollow as I've ever seen anyone.

"No," she said, lowering the fist. "There's only one way to fix this, and that's for you to show me how she does it."

"Show you ..."

"How to fuck a guy for money."

For a second, I literally thought I was about to pass out.

"Oh my god, Kaylee, no. No, I couldn't possibly – and *you* can't – your mom would never forgive me for doing it or herself for putting you in that position. I can totally give you my four-fifty and maybe some more, however much that will help, but I won't let you have sex with me for it."

Completely unmoved, she said, "Four-fifty times however many times a month is still nothing, Dennis. I mean, unless you're over here every other night at four-fifty a pop, which I assume you're not ... are you?"

"Uh, four-fifty is for the whole month."

Now it was her turn to blink. "Holy crap. She really does like you, doesn't she? Dennis, she gets three or four hundred a *session* from most of her clients. I've been going through her accounting files all day trying to figure out how fucked we are, and *that's* the kind of money I need if I'm going to make the house payment and the car and insurance and my tuition bill. Four-fifty? Jesus, she lets you have it for cheap. How many times does that get you?"

My face felt like she'd rubbed chili oil on it. "Look, I don't think that really matters ..."

"It does if you're going to understand what I'm up against. God, Dennis, are you like the most naive guy in the universe?"

"Yeah," I said, grimacing and trying not to let her push my buttons. "I guess so."

Her mouth shut and she stared at her wineglass, now half-empty. "I shouldn't have said that. I don't know why I'm bitching at you." Then she looked back up at me. "But I *do* know that I have to convince as many of Mom's clients as I can to let me stand in for her, or it's all gone. Everything she's been on her back opening her legs to keep hold of for the last thirteen years."

"Look, I know you're upset, and you can say whatever you want about me. But could you please not be crude about your mother?"

I could see her having to bite her tongue. But she did it, and after she did, her face softened a little. "Wow. You've really got it bad for her, don't you?"

"I'd do anything for her," I said without hesitation. "And if you take me to the hospital and let me see her and she says your plan really is the only way, and she wants me to help you, I will. But without talking to her, I don't want to hear another damn thing about it."

Watching her think, seeing the wheels turn behind those flaring blue eyes, I wondered whether I'd successfully called her bluff – or if there was a bluff to be called.

She finished thinking, threw back the last of the wine, and stood up.

"Okay, then. Let's go."

* * *

Neither of us talked on the drive to the hospital. In the silence, I became acutely aware of her stunning body, just turned twenty a few months earlier. *Christ, how many times has Gloria pretended to be this girl for me, and now there's the real thing sitting right there, and I'm hoping she tells me to keep my hands off it.*

Kaylee stood a good four inches taller than Gloria, slimmer through the hips ... about the same bust size. Her mother had the sexiness of a stripper wrapped up in a MILF-housewife package, but Kaylee could have been a super-model, with a magazine-cover face, unbelievably straight, rich, blood-red hair, and a body that, dressed in shorts and a t-shirt, screamed to be poured into a string bikini for an all-day photoshoot somewhere sandy and tropical.

She wasn't someone very many men would turn down.

God, I hope Gloria says she's got a rainy-day fund squirreled away somewhere.

* * *

They had the head of her bed raised, and she lay back against a pillow there, eyes closed, when I entered the room. At the receiving desk, they'd told us we had to go in one at a time, and Kaylee let me go first.

The bulk of a full-length cast made her right leg a larger bulge beneath the sheet than her left. Band-aids tracked their way up her left arm, and another one covered a cut on her forehead, smack in the middle of a huge bruise. Both her eyes had been blackened, and clearly no one had given her a brush or comb since she was admitted; her scarlet hair splayed wildly across the pillow around her head. An IV stand dripped fluid through a tube into her right arm.

She was so beautiful.

As I stepped closer, her eyelids cracked open, and a slow, happy smile lifted the edges of her mouth up. "Denny ..."

"Hi."

She tried to sit up a little, flinched in pain, dropped back against the pillow.

"Sorry," she gasped, then relaxed into a few deep breaths. Somehow the smile hadn't left her face. "Not in the best shape to make our appointment, I guess."

"It will keep."

Her hand lifted an inch or two off the blanket. I reached down and took hold of it.

"Kind of expected you to show up last night. Or on your lunch hour today."

"If I'd known, I would have gotten here before the ambulance dropped you off."

As if it took some effort to work through my words, her brows knitted and relaxed and knitted again. *They must still have her pretty doped up.*

"Kaylee ... called you. Didn't she?"

I shook my head. "No, but she brought me when I showed up at your place tonight."

The essence of fuming motherhood settled into her eyes and simmered there. "Showed up ... I told her to call you. Yesterday. Why did she go and let you ..."

"It's fine," I said, squeezing her fingers. "I really don't mind –"

Taking her hand back, she grimaced and squeaked and worked herself further up in the bed.

"Gloria, please, take it easy."

"If she didn't call you," she said, panting, "did she call anybody? I know you don't mind, but some of them ... they'll be, pissed, if they show up and I'm not ..."

Wow. Kaylee didn't come up with that idea on the fly talking to me. Gloria told her to cancel everything yesterday. And she didn't do it.

"Yeah, look ... Kaylee has this plan worked out that you're going to have to talk her out of, because I got nowhere when I tried."

She sat there for a minute, blinking, thinking. Then her hand lifted again, asking for mine. I took it.

"Shit, Denny."

"I know. I told her there had to be some other –"

Her head dropped against the pillow again, eyes closed. "No, she's totally right. Fuck me, how could I have let this happen?"

"You're not serious," I said. But the tightness of her grip in mine said she was. "There's got to be –"

"Denny." The blue of her eyes, swimming in those bruise-blackened sockets, shut me up. "You're not a dumb guy. But I'm smarter than you, and Kaylee is ... *way* smarter than I am. God. She must've ... I gave her my password, told her to call everyone, cancel ... she's been digging through my records this whole time. She can do the math. Trust me."

"But you've got equity in your house, right? You can use that to cover her tuition, then –"

"Can't get an equity loan when you're behind on your payments, honey." She glanced down at her immobilized leg. "And have no income."

"Well ... shit, sell *me* the house, and I'll get the equity loan. She doesn't have to ..."

My voice dropped off at her smile and the tears in her eyes. "Denny. What are you going to put down? That stuff with your parents ... I know you're busted."

Standing there, holding her hand and meeting her gaze, I found my brain empty of any other solutions. "Gloria, she asked me to help her."

Amazingly, she laughed at that. The tears broke free and rolled down her cheeks, and her face immediately clenched in pain, from her cracked ribs, I guess, but the laugh kept going until it looked like she couldn't breathe.

"Oh," she said, sucking in a breath at last. "Oh! God. You should have just ... said so ... in the first place."

"What do you mean? Why?"

"Denny, she asked for *help*? Kaylee doesn't ask for help, honey." Something between pride and bedevilment showed in her eyes. "Ever. If she'd go that far ... ask you to help ... she's set on it. No talking her out of it. You or me."

"So," I said, barely able to digest her words, "you're just going to let her?"

She shook her head. "Can't stop her. That's it. Unless I call the cops on her. But then we still lose it all ... *and* I go to jail. Maybe her too."

"Wow." Her hand felt so soft and sure in mine. "You seem awfully ... calm about the idea."

Rolling her eyes toward the IV stand, she got her smile back. "Drugs."

I tried to think of what else to say. Nothing came to me.

"Thank god she has you to help her."

That almost made me drop her hand. "What? No, you're not seriously –"

"Hah," she said, managing to keep it to a chuckle that wouldn't hurt her ribs. "God's sake, Denny. I know you want to fuck her. What are you trying to protect me from? I know *everything* ... you want to do to her."

"Gloria, that's different. I wouldn't really –"

She nodded. "Yeah. It's different. Know what else is different? You, compared to them. Gentle. Kind. Sweet, nervous. Good to her. Not like my first couple of tricks. God, I spent so long ... puking in the toilet after the first few times. She knows you a little. Knows how much ... *I* think of you. You want her to have that, for her first one ... or Marty Harris? 'Smy first Tuesday appointment, Marty. What I call a pump-and-grunter."

I couldn't help but make a face at that.

"Right." Her eyes slipped shut again. "We're stuck. She's gonna whore herself. You want to teach her how ... or let Marty do it? Know who *I'd* rather."

I could feel my hand getting sweaty in hers. "Gloria ..."

She looked back up at me, gave my fingers a squeeze. "Go fuck my daughter. You want to. She needs it. Enjoy yourself ... see if you can make her enjoy it too. 'f you can't ... maybe it'll change her mind. And ..."

"Yes?"

Her expression went wicked. "Tell her you're going to call her 'Brandy.'"

* * *

"Holy shit. We're really going to do this."

The whole car ride back to the house – back to the boudoir – was full of Kaylee repeating that thought or something similar.

"I can't believe she didn't go ape-shit. Fuck. Oh crap. Fuck. I'm about to have sex with you for money."

No, you're about to have sex with me because I love your mom and she needs me to do this. Assuming I can get it up. But that last bit was fooling myself. I'd been rock hard since we both shut our doors and the soft hint of her perfume spread through the interior of the car.

"Hey, why are we stopping?"

"ATM. If you're having sex with me for money, I need money, right?"

"Mom's computer ledger said you already paid your four-fifty. I figured that was just for one time, but if I'm charging what she does, you're set for the month."

"Then I'm paying for next month. If I'm going to show you what it's like to pimp yourself out, you need to know how it feels to take the cash."

"I guess so. Holy shit."

The conversation paused while I keyed in my PIN and made the withdrawal.

"Wait ... next month? Does that mean you're really going to come back and keep all your appointments, while I'm ..."

"Jesus, Kaylee, do you want to know what it's like to have a client or not?"

"Fuck. Holy crap."

We pulled into their driveway around eight o'clock, still light outside with the evening sun of early summer. I switched off the engine.

"Okay. Here's the deal," I said.

Kaylee caught me in her skeptical blue gaze, back immediately straightening at my words.

"First off, none of that."

Her eyes narrowed. "None of what?"

"*That*," I said. "No tensing up because you don't think you're going to like what I have to say. No pushing back, no sharp looks, no sarcasm. When you open that door in a minute and let me in, I'm your customer, and you act like you're happy to see me, and the things I say are intriguing and arousing."

She tried to loosen up, didn't succeed as well as she might have.

"Next," I said, raising a hand and counting onto my second finger, "you're going to need to dress yourself up before I knock on the door. Your mom's got a closet full of stuff, and I'm pretty sure she keeps notes on what to wear for who when."

"Yeah, I found that when I was digging around on the computer. Didn't have anything listed for you, though."

"I like the black silk kimono thing. I think she's known that for longer than she's had the computer." *And I guess she pays enough attention to my special requests that she doesn't have to write them down.* "But that's not what you're wearing for me, because I don't want to be comparing you to her."

"What do I wear for you?"

Flash: Gloria as Brandy bent over a laundry-basket full of things she'd borrowed from Kaylee's room, a soft, pretty blue blouse on top of the pile, the frill that would hang across the breasts stained with cum from where I'd thrown a full condom on it.

"Uh ... how about something ... blue. To match your eyes. Something frilly, if you've got it. And white shorts if you have those. The tighter the better."

"Do I need to ... like, shave or anything?"

Awesome. She's still got pubes. Wait ... Jesus, you asshole, what would Gloria think of you thinking that about her daughter? God, this is so fucked up. "No – look, we're getting deeper into the details than we need to right now." *And it's not giving me a break from my hard-on.* "Your mom and I usually go two hours, but since I'm paying you extra and you need to learn the ropes, I think we should do three. There's an alarm on the nightstand by the bed, set it for three hours and make sure it's on 'chime.'" There was a 'buzz' setting too, and it had scared the shit out of me the one time Gloria accidentally left the dial on the wrong spot.

"Three hours, chime. What else?"

"I'm going to do things in stages, okay? I'm going to start off as Nice Dennis, and hopefully when we've done a round of that, you'll be comfortable enough that I can switch to Demanding Dennis. Then if that doesn't scare you off, I'll eventually get to Dick Dennis."

"You act like a dick to my mom?" A little heat colored the question.

I raised a hand to placate her. "Not very often, and the key word there is 'act.' Sometimes we role-play. She'll pretend to be," *you*, "my boss, dressed up in a business suit."

"Your boss is a chick?"

"Yes, my boss is a woman. And she's kind of a bitch. And she's my boss, so I don't get to be a dick to her. But Gloria can put on a wig and a suit, and then I get to tell my boss the things I'd like to tell her and order her to do the things I'd like her to do to make up for how she treats me at work."

"Huh." She thought for a second, then said, "I guess I get it."

"So here's the really important part," I said. "If we get that far – hell, even if we don't get that far, but something's happening and you need me to stop, you're going to have a safe word. And if you say it, I'll stop, no matter what, right then and there. Okay?"

"I know what a safe word is," she said, a bit bristly. My eyebrows went up, and she bristled even more. "From reading smut stories online, not from being a perv myself."

"So pick one. What's your safe word."

She considered for a moment.

"Asymptote."

"No, something simpler, something you can say quicker. And something that doesn't start with 'ass.' You may be saying 'ass' for some other reason, and I don't want to have to wait and see if you're going to add 'ymptote' every time you do."

"Scorn."

I laughed. "Sure, that's good. What else? Oh – boundaries. The customer is the customer, and if you're too picky about what you will and won't do, he's not going to want to pay you. But you get to say going in what you're willing to take and what you're not. Gloria doesn't let most guys do her in the ass, for instance –"

"But you, she does?"

"– but if you're okay with taking it there, that's up to you. To start off, I'd say you should be hesitant about letting anybody tie you up. And you should definitely insist on condoms, every time for every hole. And no kissing unless you want mono or something."

"Duh. But you didn't answer my question."

"And I'm not going to. You can ask your mom if you really want to know; I'm not going to piss on her privacy."

She tilted her head a little. "Damn. You really are a nice guy, aren't you?"

"Doesn't Gloria keep telling you that?"

A shrug was all I got in response. "So what else?"

I didn't have any other instructions, but I still chewed on my lip a second. "Just ... when you open that door and let me in, remember that I'm acting, okay? Even when I start off as Nice Dennis, I'm role-playing for you, and only because of what happened to Gloria. I'm not saying I won't start enjoying things at some point; I'm not saying it's going to be a chore. But I'm nervous as hell, and I really don't – I don't want you to come out of it hating me."

"Fuck," she said, blue eyes widening, "are you going to ask her to marry you or something?"

I scowled. "Just get inside and get changed. I'm ringing the bell in fifteen minutes."

* * *

When she opened the door, I saw Kaylee completely transformed. For one thing, she was eye-level with me in a pair of three-inch white sandal heels that matched her camel-toe-tight white denim shorts. She had on the blouse, too, and I stared at her tits in it for longer than I should have. They filled the top out lushly behind the neckline fringe, pert and proud and clearly unhampered by any bra. Only as an afterthought did I look to see that the cum-stain had definitely washed out.

Her face ... well, every time I'd met her before, she'd had on very little makeup, just enough to accentuate the natural perfection of her features. Now she'd vamped it up – not in a tacky or sleazy way, but enough to make her lips a searing red and bring out the full vivacity of her eyes. I puckered as if to let out a whistle, but didn't.

"Wow. You look fucking hot, babe."

She got a smile on at that, with only a twitch of awkwardness. "Um, thanks. I guess ... you're not looking bad yourself."

Yeah, not bad-looking for a perv who's about to fuck the love of his life's daughter. But as soon as I thought that, I followed it up with, *Okay, just shut the fuck up with the guilt shit already. Gloria's fine with it. Right? She said ...* Then, what hit me was, *Did I just think "love of my life?" Holy shit.*

"So, I guess – come on in, right?" She stepped aside, holding the door wide, gesturing into the boudoir. The move looked natural enough. But before her hand dropped, I thought I spotted it shaking.

Damnit, get your head in the game. No matter how I felt about Gloria, I was here to help her and to help Kaylee, and if I blew it, both their lives could end up completely screwed. Squaring my shoulders, I said, "Sounds good to me."

As I walked past her, I caught a whiff of freshly applied perfume, something fancier and more intoxicating than the light scent I'd caught from her back in the car. It occurred to me that the earlier smell must have been her deodorant, not perfume. The state she'd been in, she obviously wouldn't have gotten up and put on perfume to start the day. Duh.

The boudoir, so familiar, usually so calming to me, seemed to crackle with unexpected static energy, threatening to zap me if I touched anything. My chest felt tight. My pants – in the crotch area, at least – felt even tighter. I put a hand behind my head, scratching the scalp there. It's very strange having to force yourself to do something you're dying to do, but that's what it took for me to turn my head and look Kaylee up and down several times as she stood waiting by the door.

"Yeah, super-hot. This is still kind of weird for me, though. You said on the phone you're taking over for your mom – does that mean you're up for anything she'd be up for?"

"Uh ..."

"No, never mind. I can tell you're new at this – I won't ask for anything freaky."

"You can tell? How?"

"Well, you look like you're about to shit yourself for one thing."

Her face reddened, her mouth opened, and her eyebrows dipped downward before she caught herself and shrugged instead of saying whatever had just popped into her mind. "Okay, yeah. I'm a little nervous. How do we get started?"

"Let's have a drink. Sit down on the couch."

For the second time that evening, I went to the tiny refrigerator and returned with wine – two glasses this time. I found her sitting very straight as far to one end of the little loveseat as its arm would let her go.

"Here." Handing her a glass, I relaxed into the other corner (well, pretended to relax), my legs angled toward the middle of the couch instead of pointing straight out like she'd left hers.

She took the glass and gulped from it.

"Whoa!" I laughed, then reached over to touch her wrist. "Let's not get you too hammered too fast."

Lowering the glass, she twitched a nervous smile my way. "Sorry."

"Don't be sorry." I sipped my own wine, then leaned to set it on the floor as I reached for my shoelaces. "I'm going to take my shoes off here."

"I'll try not to faint."

"Ha, see, that's good." My angle, as I bent, put my head almost level with her flawless white knees. I undid my laces by feel, eyes magnetized by her legs and pulled up along their clean, lush length to the point at which they entered her shorts and framed the denim-tightening curve of her mound. Then I realized where I was looking, turned my face back to my shoes and got them off.

Kaylee had her eyes awkwardly pointed at her lap when I leaned back into the cushions.

"Sorry," I said, before I could help it. "I didn't mean to be a pig. You're just – god, you're fucking amazing."

That made her smile and squirm simultaneously, but at least it got her eyes pointed back my direction. "Yeah, well ... maybe this is going to be a little harder than I thought."

"Drink some more of your wine," I said. Then, out of nowhere, I added, "And I'll tell you about the first time your mom and I did it."

"Jesus, TMI," she said, holding the palm of one hand toward me.

I laughed. "Not the filthy dirty bits. The part like this, where we were sitting drinking wine and one of us was freaking out. But in that case, it was me."

Looking at me suspiciously over the rim of her glass, she tipped it up and drank – then touched her fingertips to her mouth as a little ladylike burp snuck past her. "Oop. Excuse me."

The embarrassment seemed to do her good. I raised my glass toward her, then took a drink myself.

"So ... why were you freaking out."

"I'd never done this," I said. "Paid for sex. My whole life I thought it was sleazy and disrespectful and, well, just plain wrong. But my wife had left me six months earlier, and the sex had been bad for a year before that, and when I went out to strut my stuff with my newfound freedom, I ended up feeling shitty after every one-night stand, because I was still too hurt to go for a relationship and I felt like I was just using women as meatbags."

Her eyebrows furrowed. "Did you lead them on like you were Prince Charming? Or were they just out for a quick hookup too?"

"No, I was pretty straightforward. None of them wanted more than a night in the sack. But I still felt like a user. Like I ought to want to get their numbers, call them again, maybe ask them out for dinner and a real conversation."

Kaylee laughed and shook her head. "Dude, sometimes girls just want to fuck too. Why would you feel bad about it?"

"I don't know." I shrugged. "Maybe I'm just a romantic. Anyway, when a buddy of mine told me about your mom, I decided, 'What the hell.' If I was going to feel like a user, why not go all the way and use someone who definitely, a hundred percent for sure did not want me to call her for dinner and a movie sometime?"

"Not completely illogical, I guess." She tilted her glass up again, getting near the end of its contents. "But you got here and lost your nerve?"

Figuring I'd better keep up with her, I took another swig myself. "I wouldn't exactly say I lost my nerve. But I got pretty close. And I might have, if your mom wasn't your mom."

"What do you mean by that?" Genuine curiosity had taken over her face by this point.

"Well, she got me drinking and she got me talking ... and she kind of tucked her legs up on the sofa with us like this." I demonstrated, drawing my knees up and angling my hips. The position brought my body perpendicular to the length of the loveseat, so that I faced directly toward her. My right arm went up onto the sofa back. "Only I'm sure she made it look a lot more casual and natural than it looks on me."

The last of her wine drained away and she held the glass idly by its bell, dangling her hand off the arm of the couch. "It's a little girly. But you're sorta carrying it off. So what then?"

"She asked a lot of questions, like she cared about the things I was saying. And every once in a while, she'd shift a little – not a lot, not like she was trying to move toward me, just like she needed to reposition a bit to stay comfortable. But somehow, every time, she ended up an inch or two closer."

As I attempted to show her, she raised an eyebrow. "Dude, that was more like six inches."

"She was way better at it than I am." My hand now rested above her shoulder on the seatback. "And every inch closer she got, I realized a little more how incredibly sexy she was." I scooted again. "I mean, at that point, she was, what, maybe only five or ten years older than you are now, right? So she still had it all. Not as supermodel hot as you are, but hot and sexy aren't the same thing, and she just *poured* on the sexy."

"And then what?" she asked quietly, glancing down to where my knees all but brushed against her left thigh.

"She kept talking to me, and she got one finger in my

hair, like this." I showed her, lazily curling a lock of shimmering red around my index finger. "And she asked me some more questions, and she unfolded her leg across my knee like this." My calf inside my dress pants came to rest at the juncture of her locked-tight knees, and then she let them part, so that my left leg could hook over hers. Her breathing sped up. She looked at my knee atop her own.

"I'm ..."

"Hmm?"

Fragile-looking blue eyes came up to meet mine. "Whooh. I'm starting to think I can really do this."

I brought my hand down out of her hair to brush her cheek. "Of course you can."

Leaning outward, my fingers trailing down her throat, along her collarbone, I set my wineglass as far out from the couch as I could. Then I took hers from her loosened fingers and set it beside mine.

"What do I do?" she asked, trembling.

"Don't do anything just yet. Let me do." I brought my left hand up to rest on her right knee, my right curling the fingers around the nape of her neck, gliding the side of my thumb along her jugular to the hollow behind her earlobe. She sucked in a breath and bit her lip and closed her eyes. "You're a very beautiful woman, Kaylee. You deserve to have things done for you."

With a kneading grip, I slid my hand from her knee along her thigh, thumb questing patiently along a path toward her groin.

"To you." Simultaneously, I pressed the tip of my thumb against the fabric that stretched tight across her mound and leaned in to put my lips against her throat, behind the corner of her jaw. She gasped. I smiled and whispered, "Yes, that's good, right?" into her ear.

She nodded, quickly. I kissed my way down her neck to

the graceful slender curve of her collarbone. Lower, my thumb dipped into the right leg of her shorts, squeezed tight between fabric and thigh-flesh, pressing firmly inward, deeper, until I felt the hem of her panties. She widened her legs, slouched her hips down. My thumb rounded the corner between pant-leg and crotch, feeling the soft curve of her mons through her panties.

"Oh god," she said.

Tonguing my way down her breastbone, I tasted the salty skin within her cleavage. My right arm curved around her neck, bringing my hand downward from trapezius to clavicle to the neckline of her blouse and in.

"Aahh ..."

My thumb found the button of her clitoris, rapidly engorging. I massaged it gently, briefly, as my fingers circled her erect nipple within the blouse.

Working my mouth wetly back up to her ear, I said, "In a second here, I'm going to take my hands out of your clothes, and then if you want me to, I can get up and go to that dresser along the wall. It's got a box of oral dams in the top drawer. While I'm getting one, you could get your pants off, and then I'll come back and eat you out through it."

"Oh fuck ..." she gasped. "Are you for real? You're going to pay me for letting you do that to me?"

"What can I say?" I asked, continuing to rub her clit. "Nice Dennis is nice."

"Jesus," she said, then sucked her lip between her teeth a moment. "Okay."

Easing my hands from within her clothes, I stood up and looked her over, splayed in the corner of the loveseat, legs now apart and stretched out before her, nipples pressing hard enough against her blouse to be noticeable even through the silky blue frill. She watched me taking her in, and when I smiled she sort of involuntarily followed suit.

The black chest-of-drawers opposite the king bed took me just a couple of steps to reach. I opened the topmost one, where a bowl of condoms and the dental dams and a healthy supply of various lubes sat in neat, orderly arrangement.

"Why don't you stand up and turn around and show me how sexy you can be getting those shorts off? Just the shorts – I'd like to do the panties, if you don't mind."

"Uh, all right."

Muscles glided within the satiny skin of those pale anaconda legs as she rose. Her eyes stayed on me when she turned, face angled my direction over one shoulder – halfway between smolder and mistrust. South of that face and north of those legs, her ass swelled the confining white fabric of her shorts to water-balloon smoothness: taut and full and curved as though the laws of physics could not allow any other shape.

Swallowing hard, I stopped her as she worked at the top button of her shorts.

"Hang on a second."

"What?" The smolder in her eyes tilted further toward mistrust.

"Could you just ... I don't know, bend over for a minute before you take those off? I'm not sure I've ever seen an ass and a pair of shorts that worked together that well."

Her expression did a little sashay of gratitude and embarrassment, but she turned fully away from me and leaned into the arm of the sofa, pushing the white-clad heart of her bottom out even rounder and firmer. If the shorts had split at the seams, it wouldn't have surprised me.

"Wow. Yes. Hold that for just a second." My throat felt dry as Death Valley, and my cock screamed at me to haul it out and jerk the hell out of it *right now*. But I managed to fumble in the drawer for one of the dental dams and a bottle of lube ... and a condom. "All right, stand back up before I come just from looking at that. Holy hell, Kaylee."

When she looked over her shoulder again, her ambivalence had all gone to a glow.

"So you want me to take these off now?"

"Fuck yes."

Undoing three vertical buttons, she watched my face as I watched her slowly release the fasteners of heaven. Her zipper went down so gradually that it ticked instead of *zitz*ing. With her thumbs in the waistband, blocked from my sight by her torso, she tensed her arms to start pushing.

"No, no," I begged, moving my hands in a horizontal circle, "bring them all the way around before you do that."

She did, thumbs sharking between the waistband and her flesh, fingers trailing first down her hips, then across the high slopes of her buttocks, ending pinkie-to-pinkie in a wide-spread clutch like pale honey poured over a double dish of ice cream.

"Whoosh," I said. "Okay, I'm ready to see what you've got inside those pants now."

Nodding, she pushed and wiggled, ass rolling side-to-side as the tight denim crept downward. The hue of her flesh showed only a shade or two darker than the shorts. When her panties came into view, they were ghostly pink.

Her shorts dropped to the floor. I continued to stare.

"You want me to bend over again?"

Yes, until the timer goes off in three hours!

"No ... how about if you sit back down."

"Sure." She pirouetted around and down into the cushions, landing with her legs wide enough for me to see three different colors in her panties – the pastel pink, a textured pink-red shadow where the panties trapped her bush, and an irregular dark patch the size of a quarter, centered on the spot where her cunt pushed into the fabric.

I walked slowly toward her, stepping around our two wineglasses to stand in the V of her spread legs. Her chest moved with fast breaths as I approached. When I stopped, her eyes glanced to my left hand, which held the lube bottle and had the wrapped condom between two fingers. I tilted the hand to emphasize the rubber in its little crinkly foil package.

"I could have pocketed or palmed this while you were turned away and brought it out once I'd licked you senseless," I said. "But I didn't want to spring it on you like that ... our first time."

Her eyes stayed on the condom. Deciding whether to be alarmed? Then she met my gaze and eased her hips lower to hang her ass right at the edge of the couch.

"Thanks, I guess. But you had me at, 'licked you senseless.'"

I grinned, lowered myself to one knee and then the other, set the lube and condom down at the base of the couch. Once I unfolded the dental dam, I brushed the hem of her blouse up along her belly until it bunched together, riding her ribcage right at the breast-line. That cleared enough tummy for me to lay the latex sheet out on. Then I wrapped my hands around the backs of her thighs and leaned deep into her crotch where a few breaths of dank, musky female arousal confirmed the nature of that conspicuously located wet patch.

Tilting my head, I brought my lips a finger's breadth from her dampness and bathed her crotch in hot air from my lungs. Her thighs trembled in my hands.

Circling my hands back up to rest on her panties, I quietly said, "I'm taking these down now."

She nodded, her lower lip between her teeth again.

Backing away a little while tugging at her underwear, I made enough room for her to bring her knees together and let the bikini-briefs slip past them. She stepped out of the panties and immediately thrust her legs wide again.

My eyes didn't know where to come to rest on the wonder we'd just revealed: the unruly auburn thatch, the bulge of her mons, puffy and clean, or the glistening pink lips that peeked out surrounding her cunt-hole. I knelt again, putting my hands on my knees to make sure a finger didn't leap out to bury itself in her, or, worse yet, that I didn't grab her by the butt cheeks and haul my salivating mouth down to latch on like a lamprey.

"Here we go then," I said, surprised that my voice had any steadiness to it at all, and that my hands didn't shake wildly as I reached for the dam with one and the bottle of lube with the other. Pinching the latex sheet and thumbing open the bottle simultaneously, I felt a momentary out-of-body sensation that this was really happening. *And Gloria knows about it. And she's okay with it. I have to be dreaming.*

But the smell floating up from Kaylee's hungry cunt and the sound of her rapid breathing told me that, no, I was definitely awake, and here, on my knees between the legs of a breathtaking young woman.

Tilting the bottle, I drizzled a streamer of lubrication right onto her clit. She flinched.

"Cold?"

"Yeah. No, wait it's…"

I clicked the bottle shut, set it down, pulled the latex dam into place by its corner.

"Tingly, huh?"

"Uh-huh. Fuck, and now it's getting really hot …" Her tone said I'd definitely picked the right bottle.

Holding the top edge of the sheet in place with one hand – half-on and half-off her bush, so that those wine-

and-ginger curls tickled my palm – I tucked the rest into place across and under her, then bent to seal my lips onto the taut, smooth barrier, feeling the muted textures of her twat through its surface.

"Ohhh," she whimpered. I began to lick while simultaneously massaging the upper curve of her mons with the thumb and forefinger that I'd used to trap the dam in place. "God, that's so *good*."

I smiled against the not-quite-right tightness of the dental dam. Either Kaylee was learning *very* fast how to pump a client's ego, or I was really getting her off.

Reaching my free hand into her crotch along with my face, I got a finger past my chin and stroked up and down her crease, pressing inward just a little farther with each pass, forcing the latex shield to dimple and then glide past her slickened lips, working more and more of its thin, rubbery substance up into her cunt. By now she was groaning and thrusting with her hips, ravenous for the pressure of my tongue and the intruding shape of my finger. I started fucking the dental dam in and out of her with that one digit, its dry, wrinkled hollow clinging to my finger with each stroke. My lips and tongue kept up their efforts on the swollen nubbin of her clit, which I seemed to feel more distinctly through the latex with every lunge of her pelvis.

"I'm getting close – " she panted.

I slurped and finger-reamed her through the dam.

"Oh god, oh fuck –" She grabbed my head, fingers in my hair, and clutched me hard against her pubic arch. "Denny – Denny –"

Do it, Brandy. Come!

"*AAHHH!* Hhhh-Ohhhh – *uh!* Ahuh! *Ghuhhhhh...*"

Her back arched high off the couch. One leg came up over the shoulder of my finger-fucking hand and dragged me against her along with her hands in my hair.

"*FUUCKKK!*"

With a last, explosive gasp, she fell back, breathing like a steam train.

"Oh god, Denny. Good god."

I kissed my way up her belly, bringing squeals and jerks from her body. Nuzzling her neck, I wrapped my arms around her. Hers drew up and around me in return.

"Let me know when you've come down enough for me to fuck you," I whispered into her ear.

"Oh god."

We held each other a while, me kissing and nibbling at her throat and earlobe, Kaylee going steadily more limp until her arms fell away to either side.

"Okay," she husked. "Whenever."

Lifting up, I found her eyes closed in placid satiation.

"Correct me if I'm wrong," I said, unfastening my belt, "but this seems to be going really well so far."

"Uh-huh."

The button went next, and then I unzipped. "So ... that being the case, it may be time for me to start edging into Demanding Dennis."

She cracked one eyelid and opened her mouth as if to say something, right as I lowered my pants and shorts enough for my fiercely erect cock to pop out. Her other eye opened and her head lifted. "Geez. You're really about to fuck me, aren't you?"

"I had the impression that was the plan all along," I said.

"Yeah, but ... damn, you're *really* ready."

She had that right. I'd been hard as rebar-reinforced concrete practically since she let me in the door, and pre-cum beaded and dripped at the tip of my penis. Reaching for the condom, I said, "Guilty as charged. And

Demanding Dennis needs you to be alert and participating, not just lying there in the afterglow with your legs open."

With a sigh, she unslouched just a little and said, "All right."

I tore open the little packet and got the condom out. "No. Give me a little more enthusiasm."

An eyebrow went up, and she levered herself higher on her elbows. "What, like, 'Wow, what a penis, I really want that in me?'"

"Don't ask me," I said, rolling the rubber onto my shaft. "Think of something yourself."

"Uh ... well, that condom looks pretty hot going on. I mean, a naked dick looks better than a condom dick, aesthetically, you know? But seeing the condom roll onto it – kind of charges me up."

"Better," I said, snugging closer between her legs, my clothed erection like a compass needle pointing north. "But try not to use words like 'aesthetically' when I'm about to stuff my cock up your sex-hole. And don't say 'pretty hot,' say 'hot.' Don't say 'kind of charges me up,' say 'charges me *up*.' Now get your shirt off and let me see your tits."

She pushed up and struggled out of the blouse, saying, "I never noticed it before, but bossy men with stiffies are a real turn-on."

"Now you're getting it. That's – whoa."

Shirt off, she leaned back and gave me a perfect view of her even-more-perfect breasts. They sat high and full, with the pride of youth and the luck of good genes. Gravity tugged them down and to the sides at the moment, but did nothing to spoil their rich, round beauty. Gloria's had probably looked like that at some point, well before I'd met her – she still had a great pair of knockers, even if they'd been around the block. But I hadn't seen breasts like Kaylee's in real life since college ... hell, I wasn't sure I'd seen any that good *ever*. As I stared, she cupped a hand under each and lifted and squeezed them together, lightly tweaking the nipples between thumb and forefinger.

"So what does Demanding Dennis want me to do with these?"

"Can you get one up to your mouth?"

"What, like this?" Lifting her right breast, she craned her neck, stuck out her tongue and ran it wetly around the areola, then licked the nipple itself, which jutted out like a fingertip.

"Uh-huh. Now let me have a turn."

Her face moved back, but her hand kept the breast raised, the brown nub and puffy ring around it pointed toward me. I leaned in, sealed my lips on it, and suckled.

"Ooh!" she said – not from my tongue rolling her nipple around, but because leaning forward had bumped the tip of my cock against her mound. "Fuck, that's getting me really hot."

I kissed my way up to her neck, felt the pulse with my lips – fast enough that I knew what she was saying wasn't entirely an act.

"Open wider, then, and let me fuck you."

Her legs scissored even farther apart and brought her feet up to rest the heels on the lip of the cushion. I rose to stand on my knees, letting my cock home slowly in on the shining damp slit of her pussy.

"God damn, this is going to be good," I said.

"Fuck me like I've never been fucked."

I plunged in.

"*NGhhuh!*" she grunted as I slid all the way to my root, smacking my pubes down against her clit. "Fuck, *yes!*"

As good as that had felt, it looked even better – and pulling back out, until only the head remained in her, looked better still: the condom gleamed with her juice, and

I'd swear I could see the throb of the veins along my shaft.

"More," she insisted. I thrust again, a long, steady, heady penetration into her depths. "Yes, Denny, god, your *cock*."

I bent, latched my mouth to her tit, and started fucking.

"Ah! Ah! Ah!" she cried in time with my strokes. "Yeah, *damn*, I've never done it like this."

My tongue dueled with the engorged bead of her nipple inside my mouth. My hips drove forward and back. My cock sluiced through her, shielded from the full glory of her cunt by its latex wrapper – probably the only reason I didn't come embarrassingly soon.

"Shit, Kaylee," I gasped, releasing her nipple to pant for breath. The sound of my belt buckle clinking against the couch with every thrust made a crude, lusty soundtrack for my humping.

"Gonna come, Denny – I'm gonna come –"

That sounded a little forced to me, but I didn't care. It pushed me right up to the edge anyway.

"Ooh ... Kaylee, Kaylee ..."

"Coming! AHH, yes, *coming!*" Her heels hooked around me and tugged me in. Her hands went wildly to my back and clawed my flesh through the fabric of my shirt. "I'M COMING SO FUCKING HARD!!!"

"FUCK!" A steam boiler went off beneath my nuts, and I helplessly emptied myself into her in gouting, spasming spurts. "Uhh, hoohh, unghhh ..."

The finger talons relaxed along my back, smoothing the cloth they'd been digging through and caressing my shoulders and spine. Several more throbs weakly filled out the condom within her vagina. I lay atop her with my chin hooked over her shoulder, nose pressing into the loveseat's cushiony backrest.

"Damn, that was a *rush*," Kaylee said.

I let out a few more panting breaths. "Did you really come?"

"No. Did you buy it? I felt like I was *totally* faking you into blowing your load."

"I bought it enough," I said, shifting so that I could look her in the face and give her a grin. "Kind of a power trip, I take it?"

She nodded. "For being so Demanding, Demanding Dennis seemed pretty easy to wrap around my finger."

"Don't get too cocky. You haven't seen Dick Dennis yet."

"Well if he shows up soon, I think I can take him. Feels like I'm on a streak."

My cock pulsed again inside her. I took hold of the condom's rim and pulled out, sitting back on my heels.

Kaylee, flush with sexual success and the self-assurance of youth, really did look like she could take on the world. Which made my job as Dick Dennis way harder than my Demanding and Nice faces had been. On the one hand, I couldn't let Kaylee go into her first real trick thinking it would be as easy as what we'd just done. Maybe it *would* be, and she'd do just fine. But if this Marty guy Gloria had talked about really dumped it on her hard, her false confidence would make the crash twice as bad when he was done.

On the other hand, if I pushed too hard as Dick Dennis, I might scare her off of the business completely. Which might not be a bad thing – except that it would probably also ruin any chance of her ever trusting me again.

"What are you thinking about?" she asked.

"I'm thinking about how to how to break your streak and then rub your nose in the cum-puddle I'm going to spew out from having you service me."

Her eyes narrowed. "Dick Dennis already?"

"Don't call me that," I said, unbuttoning my shirt with sudden determination. "Call me Mister Dennis, Sir."

"Really? Because I thought Dick Dennis would want me to do some things wrong so he could teach me a lesson."

I dragged off the shirt and the undershirt too, both of them damp and the undershirt soaked from the fucking I'd just given her. Without warning, I chucked the t-shirt right at her head.

She dodged and batted it down with one hand. "What the hell?"

"Bury your face in that and suck in some deep breaths through your nose."

"Fuck, you really *are* a dick."

"*Do* it. And say, 'Yes sir, Mister Dennis, Sir.'"

Glaring, she took hold of the shirt. "Yes sir, Mister Dennis, Sir."

Her nose wrinkled as she lifted the sodden shirt toward her face. "Whew, Jesus."

When she pressed her face into the wet fabric, I slid quickly over to grab the dental dam from where it had fallen on the floor earlier. I made a pouch of it for two of my fingers, making sure I got the floor side in against them. Then, just as a little gagging noise came out of her and she started to lower the shirt, I lined my fingers up and jammed them all the way into her cunt.

"Agh! Fuck!" she jerked and dropped the t-shirt and tried to wriggle away, but I kept the pressure on and followed her hips, vibrating my fingers inside her.

"*Hold still.*"

She stiffened and sat there. With her hips no longer trying to squirm out of reach, I was able to start finger-fucking her with the oral dam. After a minute or so of squelching, slippery finger sex, she said, "I'm really not liking this."

"You're not supposed to like it. *I'm* supposed to like it. That's your job, right? Letting me do things to you that get me off."

"I guess," she said sullenly. I reached up and tweaked a nipple. "Ow! Hey!"

"How do you say it? Not 'I guess.'"

Through clenched teeth, she replied, "Yes sir, Mister Dennis, Sir."

"Good." I kept hand-reaming her for a while as we stared at each other. *Fuck. What's going on in her head? Is she remembering this is an act? Is* she *putting on an act for Dick Dennis? Am I making her hate me?*

One thing was for sure: I wasn't going to get hard again from this situation.

Pulling my fingers out, I shook the dental dam loose so that it flapped lubily to the floor. "Okay, enough foreplay for you. Now it's time for you to get me warmed up. Go get a couple more condoms."

"Yes sir, Mister Dennis, *Sir.*" She got off the couch like she couldn't get far enough away from me fast enough. While she retrieved the condoms from the dresser, I stood up and got my pants the rest of the way off, then my socks. My dick hung limply between my legs, the cum-filled rubber still dangling from it. I walked over to the bed, flung back the sheets, and climbed onto the mattress on my knees.

Kaylee turned and took a step toward me, looking nakedly vulnerable but also defiant.

"Wait," I said, putting up a hand. "Get some lube too. Gel, not the liquid."

As she turned back to the drawer, I admired her back and her ass. Still not a twitch from my dick, though.

"Put those on the nightstand," I said as she reached the foot of the bed with two condoms and a tube of gel. Then

I patted the sheets in front of me. "I want you on your back here for a minute."

She did what she was told, though without another *Yes sir, Mister Dennis, Sir.* I was actually just as glad for that – it made me feel like shit.

Settling in on her back, she forced her gaze up at me, which meant she couldn't avoid seeing my pendulous cock and its spew-swollen rubber. I moved closer so that it drooped directly above her left shoulder.

"Take this off me."

She screwed up her face, but lifted a hand and tugged at the condom, then brought her other up to unroll it a bit until it slid loose.

"Now pour it onto your tits and smear it around."

"Ew."

"What?"

Gruffly, she said, "Yes sir, Mister Dennis, Sir."

It took her a couple of false starts before her nerve let her upend the latex tube and drip the gloppy leavings of our earlier sex onto her chest. Flipping the condom away, she brought her hands down to her breasts and began massaging my cum across them.

"Yeah, that's it," I said, watching her squeeze and knead herself, frosting her bosom with ejaculate. Despite my unease at treating her this way, it was a really hot sight, and at last I felt a hint of an erection stir. "Okay, now we're talking."

I leaned across her – forcing her to twist her neck to keep my still-wet cock from slapping a cheek. From the nightstand, I grabbed one of the condom packets and ripped it open. Sitting back on my heels, I maneuvered the disc into place and unrolled it quickly along my still-soft but thickening prick. Then I knelt over her head and offered it to her.

"Suck."

She opened her mouth with a look of disgust, then lifted it to surround my cockhead. The tender touch of her lips worked like magic to stiffen me up. I thrust down while I watched her continue to play with her boobs, the coating of semen now rapidly drying to a sticky mess.

Holy shit, that feels good, I thought, still feeling guilty, but with the physical pleasure starting to push that emotion back into the shadows. Kaylee bobbed her head up to swallow me in slow strokes – her eyebrows furrowed and the tendons of her neck standing out. It obviously wasn't a comfortable position for her to be blowing me from. But that didn't matter because I quickly got back to full erection, at which point I withdrew from her mouth and flipped around to get between her legs.

"I don't think I'm ready," she said in an unhappy tone. "Are you going to use the lube?"

For a second I considered working up a dollop of spit and dropping it right onto her snatch. But Dick Dennis was only supposed to be a dick within the confines of the rules, which said no mixture of bodily fluids and orifices.

"If you want it, you get it," I said instead.

I'd already lowered myself over her, which forced her to strain to reach the nightstand. I could have shifted to make it easier on her, but I didn't. My only compromise was to lift up my hips so she could reach between us and slather the gooey gel onto the condom around my dick.

"As long as you're down there, guide me in," I said.

She stared up at me, said, "Yes sir, Mister Dennis, Sir," and brought the tip of my penis into alignment with her hole.

I went in fast and rough, the overdone coating of lube making the glide smoother than I intended, although it still brought a glottal sound of discomfort from her.

What had Gloria called the Marty guy? *A pump-and-grunter. Right.*

Pressing my weight against her, I grabbed her shoulders with both hands and began to thrust. On every in-stroke, I squeezed an animal noise from my throat – a pleasureless rutting sound with no happiness to it, only an insistent demand for orgasm.

"Uh, uh, uh," I panted and plunged, mechanically, ceaselessly, without variation. "Uh, uh, uh."

Kaylee lay motionless beneath me. I had my mouth in next to her ear, so I couldn't see what kind of expression she wore. After several minutes of vulgar thrusting, I broke my scratched-record grunting to say, "How's *that* feel, huh?"

"I don't like it, De– Mister Dennis. Sir." The quaver in her voice sounded more real than I wanted it to.

"Uh, uh, uh, what, is my cock not big enough for you? Uh!"

"No, it's big ... Sir."

"Uh, uh, uh, is it not hard enough?"

"No, Sir, it's hard. It's just ..."

"Uh, uh, uh."

"It's ..."

"Uh, uh – wait." I lifted up, no longer humping. "I know."

Shame and disgust were written all over her face. "You do? What?"

"It's in the wrong hole. You need it in your ass."

Her eyes shot wide. "Oh my god, no."

"Yeah, you need to be buttfucked hard until you scream." Quick as I could, I pulled out and wrestled her over onto her stomach.

"No, really, no, stop ..." She twisted and writhed, but my weight had her pinned in place, and I ground the sloppily lubed bar of my cock between her ass-cheeks. "Dennis, no –"

I worked a hand between us, repositioned my dick, found the dimpled entrance to her bottom with its tip.

"Oh yeah, this is gonna be good. Get ready for it, baby."

"No, Dennis – *SCORN!*"

I was off her in a heartbeat, electric relief shooting from my chest out through my arms.

"Oh, thank god, Kaylee, I thought I was going to have to stop and remind you."

She froze, having scrambled halfway off the bed, her breathing wild and eyes wilder. As my words sunk in, the panic subsided to mere anxiety.

"You ..."

"Are you okay? I could tell you were at least a little scared but I didn't know how much of it might be an act, and I didn't know whether you remembered about the safe word."

Searching my face – which I hoped looked as concerned as I felt – she untensed, at least slightly. "If I hadn't said it, you wouldn't have ..."

"God, no," I said, looking down at my dick, which had shriveled completely by this point. "I was already losing my hard-on when I pulled out of your pussy. It wouldn't have gone in even if I'd tried. Which I promise you, I was never going to do."

She put her face in her hands, shuddering. "Oh my god."

"Would it help if I came over and held you?"

Instead of answering, she rushed up and into my arms, tears rolling down her cheeks. "Dennis, I was so scared."

"I'm sorry, baby." I stroked her hair and rocked us back and forth. "I'm sorry."

"What if – what if one of them does something and I say the word and he doesn't stop?"

"They all stop, Kaylee." I'm not sure I sounded or felt very convinced of that, but I went on anyway. "Gloria's only told me about one time where she even had to say her word more than once."

"But what if they don't?"

"Do you know how to shoot a gun? I'll show you where your mom's got one and a can of mace."

She pulled back and looked at me, bright blue eyes finding something in my face that they hadn't seen there before. "Jesus. You really wanted me to know what I was getting into, didn't you."

I nodded and brushed a strand of red hair from her cheek, where tears had stuck it to the skin. "Yeah. I've never been that ugly with your mom, no matter what we were role-playing. But I know she has some clients who get off on being shitty."

"Whoosh." Her breathing had calmed down. She looked drained and exhausted now, but no longer petrified. "I guess that's a good thing. After Nice Dennis – and even Demanding Dennis – I was thinking, 'What the hell am I going to school for? Mom was right, this is really a pretty good job.'"

I kissed her forehead. "Well, I knew it was crappy of me to be Dick Dennis with you. But I thought it would be even crappier to give you the wrong impression about what things were really going to be like."

A muddled, half-grateful look came over her, but she didn't talk. Instead, she just nestled her face back in against my shoulder. I held her for a while in silence.

"So," I said, when I thought enough time had passed. "Now that you have the whole picture, do you know what you're going to do? Do you really want to go through with it?"

"Well," she said, "I don't quite have the *whole* picture, do I?"

"What do you mean?"

Shifting to look at me, she raised one hand and rubbed the fingers together. "I still don't know what it's like to get paid."

I smirked. "That part usually happens when I'm dressed and ready to leave. Give me a second to get my clothes on."

But as I started to move away, she grabbed my arm. "I don't think that's going to work."

"What do you mean?" Her grip on my bicep, her tone, and the look on her face all seemed like they should be telling me something, but I didn't get it.

"I mean, you're not Nice Dennis or Demanding Dennis or Dick Dennis anymore. You're not Client Dennis at all. You're Denny, my mom's friend who brought us Thanksgiving dinner, who for some reason really cares about what happens to me even though I've only ever been crappy to him. All it's going to feel like taking your money is that I finally understand you're a really good guy."

That warmed something up inside me, but I could tell she meant more by it than just an expression of gratitude. "Okay, well, I guess I screwed up the payment part. I don't know what to do about that, though."

She looked at me like I was stupid, which actually felt more comfortable and familiar than the soft, appreciative look she'd had a moment before.

"You don't? I thought it was pretty obvious you have to fuck me again," she said. "As Nice Dennis or Demanding Dennis though. I don't need any more Dick Dennis lessons."

"You're serious."

Glancing at the clock, she said, "We're still way under three hours, and I need to hold some whore money in my hands. I can't know for sure what I'm going to do without that."

"Wow." I should have felt guilty, that it would be wrong to take advantage of what she was asking. But what I felt instead was my cock starting to stand back up. "Then ... Nice Dennis or Demanding Dennis?"

"Demanding Dennis, I think," she said. "There can't be all that many Nices on Mom's client list, and I bet none at all as nice as you. Demanding Dennis is probably better practice."

That's a really good point.

"Right, then. Uh, is there anything else you want to say before I go back into, uh, client mode?"

"Yeah." She leaned in and kissed me on the cheek. "I'm really glad my mom knows you."

I flushed, blood surging in both my face and my groin. "Thanks. That's really sweet of you."

"You're welcome. And now Sweet Kaylee is signing things over to Slut Kaylee. What does Demanding Dennis want Slut Kaylee to do?"

"Nothing," I said. "Demanding Dennis says your name is Brandy for the rest of tonight. And Demanding Dennis wants you to go wash that other guy's cum off your chest and then come back and ride him cowgirl style while he gropes that fantastic rack of yours. Incidentally, Brandy is pretty surly and resentful about having to fuck Demanding Dennis. She feels like he's taking terrible advantage of her. But she always comes anyway."

"Sure," she said, reaching in to pat my erection. "I'll be right back."

While I lay on my back and the tap ran in the powder room, I wondered what Gloria might be thinking about this, right now, in her hospital room. *Assuming she's not knocked out from the pain meds.* I couldn't figure it out for sure, but apparently my cock was convinced she wouldn't be thinking anything bad, because it stayed pointed straight up the whole time Kaylee was in the bathroom.

After a few minutes, she returned, breasts pink and dry from a fresh scrubbing. I ordered her to put the condom on me, and then she crawled onto the bed and into place atop me.

"God, Brandy," I told her. "Your body is *so* fine."

"Yeah, sure. Let's just get this over with."

She angled herself, then slid down onto me and began to grind.

"Oh, yeah. *Fuck* me like that, baby."

"I'm fucking," she grumbled. "Doesn't it feel like I'm fucking?"

Her cunt drooled so wetly along my shaft that I felt the fluid running past the condom and into my pubic hair.

"It sure does. Push your tits out for me."

She arched her back, lifting and emphasizing her amazing breasts. I put my hands up to them, clutched and rolled them around, marveled at their richness, fullness, softness. The slide and stroke of her crotch against mine, her vagina around the tower of my dick, matched the rhythm of my kneading as she stared coolly down at me.

"You look like you want to bitch at me about something," I said, stifling a groan as she hit a particularly good downstroke.

She folded her lips in as if to wet them before speaking. "I just always wonder why a dirty old fuck like you thinks it's okay to make a nice college coed whore herself to him."

"Ha," I said, then, "Oh, yeah, keep doing that. Mm-hmm. Why? Because I can, sweetheart. Because a dirty old fuck like me is never going to get a nice college coed to be his girlfriend, so I might as well settle for the next best thing."

For a second, something soft in her face looked like she might argue with me about whether a nice college coed would want to be my girlfriend. Then she hardened up her features and said, "Damn right. In fact, I don't know how a dirty old fuck like you could get any girlfriend at all. The best thing that's ever going to happen to you is if you get to be with a really nice whore."

I couldn't help smiling at that, even though it pushed me totally out of character. Kaylee sped up her motions, screwing me with delicious, quick rolls of her hips.

"You like that idea, huh? Some really sweet, smart, funny whore who'll get you off and act like you're some kind of gentleman and make you wish you really deserved her. Well, dream on, you nasty prick. *Nff* ... ohh ... but – but if you ever find her, all I can say is, if you find her, gnhh – *shit* – you damn well better treat her better than you treat me."

She gave up the act then and just fucked me, face squeezed tight in the heat of sexual frenzy. "Fuck ... oh, fuck, Dennis ..."

"Yeah, Brandy. That's it ... ooh, that's it ... who's a good girl? Who ... ahhh – who needs some cum up her snatch?"

"*Uhhh*, god. Uhh, god, I'm coming ..."

"Shit, me too, Brandy – do it, girl, do it –"

"AH-AHAH – AHHH!" She curved backward, making an almost perfect semicircle from her throat down her chest and along her belly. "*YE-EHSSS* ..."

A squeezing pulse of orgasm tremored through her cunt, pushing me over the edge. I cried out her name – her real name, *Kaylee* – unable to help it as joy ricocheted through my body to burst loose as a fountain of bliss inside her. Up and up I shot my ecstatic wonder, burning through my entire form as this gorgeous young woman rode me to a peak of love – love for her, love for her mother, a crazy tangle of love and sex that shivered through me and tried its best to fill her from belly to braincase.

Then, done, she fell down onto me, trembling, and I wrapped my arms around her and held her. She didn't pull away until the chime sounded, by which time she'd recovered enough to get back in character.

"Okay, time's up, prick," she said, rolling away so that my condom-covered dick flopped out onto my belly. "Get up and get dressed and give me my damn fuck money."

I groaned and rose from the bed, slowly, every inch of me fighting the need to leave that place of pure, warm comfort behind. It took most of the time I spent dressing to get my head together and work at playing my part right.

"Sheezus," I breathed, tugging out my wallet once I had everything on. "You really wore me out, you little hussy. For such a prissy tight-ass, you sure can fuck."

"You should kick in some extra, then," she sneered. "Except we both know you're too cheap to do that."

"You'd only waste it on some college learning, darling. Why would I encourage you to go and do that when you're so good at blowing and boning? Here. Four-fifty. While you're spending it, think about all the fucking it's going to get me over the next month."

I slapped the money into her hand, then watched as she unfolded and slowly counted it.

"Holy shit," she breathed.

"That's right, honey. You earned it all. Your momma would be proud."

She looked up at me then, and a brief moment of tension held us both suspended. Not being in her head, I couldn't tell for sure what went on with her during that moment, but for me, it was a fight against an overwhelming desire to grab her up in a hug and not let her go all night.

Then the moment passed, and she snarked, "My momma *will* be proud. And don't think I'm not going to tell her all about it. Now there's the door."

I got my feet in motion, unlatched and opened the door. Then, with one shoe in and one shoe out, I turned back and mimed a tip of a hat to her.

She rolled her eyes and waved me away, and I shut the door behind me.

* * *

I was at the hospital by quarter of nine the next morning, waiting for visiting hours to start. When the floor's receiving nurse let me in, I went straight to Gloria's room with a moderately giant arrangement of flowers. She laughed when she saw them.

"Oh, those are perfect, Denny," she said. Her voice and her laugh both sounded tired, but whole. "Not too small to make a girl feel better, but not so big that she starts to wonder if you're trying to make up for an indiscretion."

I cleared my throat and brought the flowers in, finding a spot on the bedside table to set them.

"You look good," I said, which was completely untrue in the sense that her eyes still had sickly dark bruise rings around them and the cuts and bandages and disarrayed hair remained as they'd been the day before. But it was also completely true in my heart. And it made her laugh again, which meant it was the right thing to say.

"You look good too," she replied. "If I wasn't so doped up on pain pills, I'd make you get in this bed and fuck me, cast and all."

I glanced over at the door, then stepped close and leaned down where I could say, without fear of being overheard, "Well it's good you're on the pills, then, because I didn't bring any condoms. Kaylee and I used protection, but the rules still say I'm out of the no-condom club for a couple months, right?"

That made her laugh even harder, until her eyes rolled up and one hand went to her ribs. "Oh, ow, ow. Haha ..."

"Are you okay? I guess I'm even funnier than I thought."

She slumped in the bed, hand still on her ribcage. But the smile stayed on her face. "Oh, Denny. You don't *seriously* believe there was ever a no-condom club, do you?"

My face went red, and I just scratched behind my head.

"So. Kaylee called me this morning, but I'm not going to tell you what she said until you tell me how it was," she said. "And you should pull up a chair, because I want details."

"Uh ..." I'd expected her to want me to say something, but I hadn't expected a detailed grilling. Suddenly all my moments of discomfort and guilt from the night before came back in a rush. "Details? That's not going to ... I mean, you really want ..."

"There's no porn channel on my TV in here, and two of my favorite people in the world had sex last night – why *wouldn't* I want to hear about it?" She pointed to a chair in the corner. "Besides, I'm pretty much the nosiest mother in the world."

Dragging the seat over, I sat down and tried to think how to start.

"Well, umm ..."

"Don't think about it so much," she said. "First off, was it good?"

I met her eyes. They said she genuinely wanted to know.

"Parts of it were incredible," I said honestly. "And parts of it were absolutely awful."

"Give me the awful parts first, so I can tell you not to worry about them."

With a deep breath, I told her about moving from Nice Dennis to Demanding Dennis to Dick Dennis, giving her a full description of the last of those and how terrible it had been to treat Kaylee the way Dick Dennis had. She nodded grimly through most of it, but when I was done, she looked relieved.

"You couldn't have done better if I'd written down a playbook for you," she said, reaching a hand out, palm up, toward me. I took it and held it and she went on, "Don't feel bad about it – any of it. You did exactly what she needed you to do."

I shrugged, a little less guilt-crushed, but not feeling entirely absolved. "Sure, but I can't help feeling bad. I was –"

"No, you weren't," she said. "You were careful and deliberate and concerned. Forcing yourself to do unpleasant things doesn't make you unpleasant, Denny. It just shows what you're willing to go through for other people. If you'd spent the whole time being Nice Dennis to her, *that's* something you'd need to feel bad about."

"I guess."

She patted and squeezed my hand. "Don't guess. Do you think Dick Dennis scared her off?"

"No," I said, shaking my head. "She texted me while I was on the way home, asking if I would come today and listen from inside the house so that she'd feel safer for her first couple of appointments. I promised to be there by eleven. She didn't tell you?"

For a second, Gloria looked away – almost as if she wanted to keep something from showing in her face.

Uh-oh. What's going on?

When she looked back, her expression was   ...

anticipatory. But I couldn't tell if she anticipated something positive or something negative.

"Well," she said after a deep breath. "There's good news and there's bad news about that. Which one do you want to hear first?"

"Shit. I hate good news, bad news. I don't know. Just pick one."

"Okay. Here it is, then. I guess after she texted you, she sat down to call Marty Harris and the rest of today's appointments, to let them know she was taking my place. And –" Her voice kind of choked off. She had to start again. "And after she told Marty about the drunk in the Hummer running me off the road, she opened her mouth to tell him she'd keep the appointment for me, and ... and she couldn't."

Something electrically happy and horrified zapped me in the chest and ran out my arms to the fingertips. *Oh thank god she won't – but Christ, what's going to happen? The bills, Kaylee's tuition ...*

Gloria went on, "She just froze up. She'd spent the whole night, after you left, thinking she could, but when the moment came, it hit her and she said she just about yarked. All she could do was apologize to Marty and tell him how sorry she was about it and how sorry I was about it. And apparently, Marty was *pissed*."

"What?" My relief and worry sizzled away into anger, and I had to work not to clench my hand too hard around Gloria's. "What kind of a –"

But she laughed. "No, Denny, he wasn't pissed at me or at Kaylee. He was pissed at the guy who hit me – for hurting me and for screwing up his appointment schedule for the next couple of months."

Now I just felt puzzled. "Okay. But what –"

Her eyes sparkled. "I think I told you Marty's not much

of a talker, right? Well it turns out one of the things he never talked about during all of his not talking was, he's a personal injury lawyer. He started cursing a blue streak about the asshole in the Hummer, saying he could probably get me a couple hundred grand as a settlement, easy. He even said he'd front me some of it to keep us afloat until I got back on my feet."

I just blinked for a while, holding her hand in mine. If she hadn't been hurt I would have grabbed her up and whirled her around the room. As it was, all I could do was look at her, half a smile on her lips, eyes looking a little teary with – relief? Pride at Kaylee for not prostituting herself? Gratitude for me ... or for Marty Harris? *Jesus, this is the guy she called a "pump and grunter" and all of a sudden he's some kind of guardian angel?*

"Do you think he really means it?"

"Oh, he means it. Marty may not talk much, but he's probably the most straightforward person I've ever met. If he says he's going to take that drunk to the cleaners, he's damn sure going to do it."

I shook my head, only half believing. Then I had another thought, and I looked more closely at her.

"So ... if that's the good news, what's the bad news?" *Did the doctors find something else they didn't notice the first time? Did Kaylee decide to hate me after all for all the things I did?*

Moving her left hand over on top of mine, Gloria said, "You're off my client list, Denny."

I waited, stock-still, trying not to hope that she meant what I wanted her to mean by that.

"Sunday night *hurt*," she said, knocking on the hard surface of her cast beneath the sheet, then running her fingers up and across her ribs. They didn't stop there, though. They kept moving up, to the center of her chest, where she pressed her hand flat staring at me. "And this is where it hurt worst. I was lying there, screaming from the pain, sure I was going to die, just kicking myself over and over again. Because whenever I blinked away the stars and had a second that wasn't agony, all I could think was, 'Oh no, Denny. He's never going to hear me say it. He's never going to get to be with me as me. I'm going to die, and all I ever gave him was the whore part of myself.'"

As always, I couldn't help lowering my eyebrows when she said that word. "That's *not* all you ever gave me."

"Of course it isn't, sweetie," she said, reaching up to my cheek. "I didn't say I was *rational* when I was thinking that. But it's the most awful I've ever felt, and I'm not ever going to let myself feel that way again."

"So you could handle ... us being together? And still do what you do?"

"Good god," she laughed. "If you can handle it, *I* sure don't have any excuse for not being able to."

"But you said before – I mean, you didn't actually say, but you *implied* ..."

"Yeah. I was scared." She looked like the admission lifted something off her. "You've been hurt, Denny, and I've been hurt. But bleeding there in that mangled mess of my car, with glass in my head and maybe a chance I wasn't ever going to see you again, I realized there's way worse ways of being hurt. And missing out on you is definitely a worse hurt than whatever's going to happen if I let you in."

I couldn't say anything to that. It was like every dream I'd ever had coming true.

Gloria squeezed my hand until it all but hurt.

"I love you, Denny."

The world seemed to float and flicker around me. For a second, everything turned the blue of her eyes. All I could manage was a whisper:

"I love you too."

Then she smiled, and I leaned and kissed her, and everything was good.

ABOUT THE AUTHOR

Ian Saul Whitcomb lives somewhere in the middling Central Time Zone of the U.S.A. He apologizes for any inaccuracies in the portrayal of prostitution in this book, as he has never actually paid for sex and couldn't convince his wife that doing so would fall under the category of "field research."

He can be found blogging at www.bigheartednarcissist.blogspot.com and on Twitter at @coolgasmic.

www.ingramcontent.com/pod-product-compliance
Lightning Source LLC
Chambersburg PA
CBHW060433130626
46555CB00005B/2340